Finding Rosie's Granddaughter

A Rosie Castro Mystery

John Buchak

This novel is a work of fiction. Names, places, characters and locations are a product of the author's imagination and are pure fiction. Any resemblance to actual persons, living or dead, events, or locales is entirely coincidental.

Cover Design: Karin Buchak

Photos by www.dreamstime.com

ACKNOWLEDGEMENTS

To my family and friends, who have given me years of support while I sat typing and retyping ideas for one novel after another.

To my sister, who tried over and over to explain how I needed to work on my self editing and finally had to jump in and help me before I pulled out the few remaining hairs I had left on my head, thank you Carol.

To my daughter, who helped me with the printing and cover ideas when I just wanted to toss up my hands and give up on finding the picture I wanted, thank you Karin.

To my granddaughter who read my first draft and told me to keep going and couldn't wait to read the finished story, thank you Courtney.

To my friend Rick Rofman, who has come to my aid on each novel I write. Thank you my dear friend for all of your help.

To P Chester Daley, wherever he may be.

1

On a warm sunny afternoon in a seemingly safe section of Brooklyn, New York, eight-year-old Lisa Soto was enjoying herself bouncing her new red rubber ball against her front porch steps when she missed catching it and it rolled to the curb. The ball wedged itself between the curb and the tire of an old Buick Roadmaster that had parked there earlier. Getting down on all fours, the young girl was trying to dislodge the ball when an old man walked up behind her. The stranger quickly placed a hand firmly over Lisa's mouth as she tried hard to scream.

The hand that had been placed over Lisa's mouth and nose contained a chloroform-soaked rag that rendered her unconscious almost immediately.

Although the neighborhood was sometimes well traveled, it was not on this afternoon. There were no people walking the sidewalks or watching out of their windows. The normal neighborhood snoops must have been busy watching their favorite soap opera or game show.

The child was loaded into the back seat of the old green four door sedan by her abductor, a man about sixty who showed no emotion. The driver, an older woman, drove off down the street at a very slow speed trying not to draw any attention to the vehicle.

The building where Lisa lived with her mother Juanita Soto was an old converted brownstone that years earlier had been condemned then partially remodeled. There was no green grass yard to speak of and the basement still had an occasional rodent problem from the overflowing garbage cans. The landlord of the building had been notified, but to no avail, of the unsafe conditions that children were forced to play in. He had contracted laborers who had started working on the clean-up and painting of the building, but all his crew had completed was to paint the handrails and the red primer on the front door.

Although it had been only a short while until Lisa's disappearance was noticed each minute that followed seemed like an eternity to her mother once discovered.

Not far from the abduction site, Rosie Castro, the little girl's grandmother, unaware of the situation, sat in the locker room of a workout gym where she didn't want to be.

Working out at the gym had become a twice-weekly regimen for Miss Castro. Her workout consisted of walking through the front door of the popular health spa and saying good morning to everyone she saw on her way to the locker room. She then changed into her workout outfit, which made her look the part of being physically involved with the equipment at hand. In reality the only physical activity she involved herself with was doughnut eating, coffee drinking, and an occasional sip from her hip flask.

The only reason Miss Castro even attended the facility was because her daughter Juanita told her, "Mom, if you don't get off your butt and start living life in a healthy way again, Lisa and I will not call or visit you in that dungeon you call home ever again."

It had been several years since Rosie was a vibrant and active member of this or any community. At forty-six years old and feeling washed up and rung out, Miss Castro had no desire to fit back into society. During her short lifetime fate had played a big hand in her downward spiral.

It was only twenty years earlier that Cadet Rosalita Carmella Castro entered the Police

Academy in Newark, New Jersey, and had very high expectations for her future.

Officer Castro moved up slowly through the ranks, pulling some of the worst duty a rookie could get, mostly because of her female attributes in a male environment. Intestinal fortitude and a driving desire to become the best police officer she could possibly be kept her pushing for that goal. After many years of working with different partners, she earned the respect she highly deserved, and was trusted by all who knew her, male and female alike.

Reaching the rank of Detective third grade in the Newark Homicide Division, there wasn't an officer in her division who wouldn't work side by side with her and she was well on her way to become the highest ranking woman in her division. It took only one extremely bad day for her world to come tumbling down.

During a routine investigation of a homicide suspect in a run-down tenement building in a tough drug infested area of Newark, Rosie was shot.

The shooting had absolutely nothing to do with the investigation she and her partner were assigned to. A crack-head drug addict, who thought the police were coming after him, saw a uniformed officer and detective in the hallway and fired several rounds from a weapon he had just stolen from a drug dealer he had robbed in the building.

Although the shooter was shot and killed by the officer, two of the drug addict's bullets found their way into the left knee and right shoulder of Detective Castro.

It took many months of rehabilitation, following a few extensive surgeries, before Rosie could walk on her own without crutches or the aid of a cane. The shooting unfortunately ended the seventeen-year career of one of the finest officers on the force. Rosie, born to Puerto Rican parents and a wonderful role model for her gender and ethnicity, was forced to, reluctantly, retire.

Moving to Brooklyn, New York to live closer to her daughter Juanita and granddaughter Lisa, was a decision made by Juanita Soto and not by Rosie.

Locating a one-bedroom apartment only two blocks away from her daughter was Juanita's idea. Rosie had so much assistance with everything in her new life she just let it happen, to the point where she started doing nothing for herself.

After a while, Juanita realized how much her mother was depending on her to do everything, no matter how small or mundane the task.

Seeing what her mother had become was very disturbing to Juanita, so she enrolled her at the local gym to try to put some activity in her life again.

Things appeared to be going fine for Rosie at least on the surface, but the reality was that the one-time vibrant ex- police detective saw nothing in what she was doing to make her existence any better and her alcohol consumption started becoming a big part of her life.

Late on that Sunday afternoon, after returning home from the gym, Rosie sat sipping on a beer, watching an old movie on TV when she received a call from Juanita. Her daughter was frantic because she couldn't locate Lisa.

After questioning Juanita, Rosie found out that Lisa had been gone for over two hours. Rosie told her daughter to call the police department and report Lisa's disappearance immediately.

A thorough search of the neighborhood by the police revealed that Lisa was nowhere to be found. A tri-state alarm went out with the description of the little girl.

Each day that passed was like an eternity to Juanita and Rosie. Then, exactly one week later, on the following Sunday, Juanita received a phone call from an unidentified man, claiming to be holding Lisa, and asking to talk with Detective Castro, and no one else.

After much crying and screaming into the phone, Juanita explained to the caller that her mom lived two blocks away and she would have to be brought to the phone, but it would take time.

The caller said, "I will call back in one hour, go get her."

Once again screaming to talk with her daughter, Juanita was told by the caller, "Stop wasting time and get Detective Castro to the phone." And then the call ended.

The FBI, who were hooked up and monitoring the call, could only say that the call came from an untraceable phone and they could not pinpoint the location.

They all agreed that something the caller said was very interesting and a definite lead in the case. The lead agent pointed out that Juanita's mother was referred to as Detective Castro, and not Miss Castro.

2

As the old Buick Roadmaster traveled west on Route 22 in the far western part of New Jersey, but attracted no unusual or unwarranted attention as it approached Pennsylvania.

In the passenger seat a middle aged woman around fifty-five was knitting what appeared to be a pink sweater. Now driving the monster of a car was the well groomed old man who was about sixty. He hummed along to the old songs playing on the radio.

Two children sat in the back seat keeping each other amused, one by coloring in a Peter Pan coloring book and the other by playing with a Barbie doll and an assortment of doll clothes. Both little girls for the past week had been given mild sedatives and even now on this trip had ingested Valium in a small dosage to keep them in a confused and somewhat sedated state. The second child had also been kidnapped and her family was suffering just as Juanita and Rosie.

As the group crossed over the state line into Pennsylvania, the woman motioned with her hand for the man to pull the car over at a roadside vegetable stand and said, "Brian, it's time for you to make your phone calls."

Without speaking a word, the driver pulled off the road and parked next to a run-down produce stand. He got out of the car, started walking and proceeded to make a call on his cell phone.

The woman in a very motherly fashion told the children, "Kids, let's get out of the car and see what kind of delicious fruits we can buy for our trip."

As the man walked around to the side of the building to a secluded location, he made his second phone call carefully reading the numbers typed out on a folded piece of paper. On the third ring, Juanita Soto answered and said, "Hello," and immediately started crying.

3

Adolpho Castro, the late husband of Rosie, had died at the hands of a bank robber nine years earlier in New York City. While making a deposit the late Mr. Castro had been taken hostage along with fifteen other innocent customers in the bank. He along with one other man was killed by the bank robbers in a show of power. The bank robbers were eventually shot and killed as they tried to escape after a ten hour standoff.

Rafael Soto, Juanita's husband and the father of Lisa, was an uncontrollable alcoholic. He had disappeared less than a year after Lisa's birth and has never been heard from. The department of missing persons had been notified but there was never any progress in the case. Juanita suspected that her husband had returned to the town of his birth in Mexico but he could not be located.

The absence of a male presence in the two households had left all decisions to be made by two very competent women, but the recent abduction of Lisa has turned even the most stable nerves to jelly.

When the phone call came from the man holding her granddaughter, Rosie reverted back to her days on the police force, and with the advisement of the FBI she listened carefully and asked specific questions.

The caller made it clear that first he would be the one asking questions, and second that Rosie would never see her granddaughter again if she did not cooperate.

Rosie, ignoring the caller's demands asked questions anyway. She asked, "What is it that you want and where is my granddaughter?"

He said, "I won't tell you again detective, I do the talking and you do the listening."

Then, trying only to act like a distraught grandmother, Rosie started crying into the phone, meanwhile giving the FBI additional time to locate where the call was coming from.

He told her, "I know what you're doing detective, and it won't work. Just know this. Your granddaughter is safe for now, but that could change. You will hear from me when I see fit to call again with my demands."

The phone connection was broken, and Rosie looked at the FBI agent trying to trace the call and asked, "What did you get?"

He said, "Sorry Ma'am."

Rosie told him, "Agent, that is not an acceptable answer."

The agent said, "Sorry ma'am, all I can tell you is that it was made from out of state."

4

After stopping at the roadside vegetable stand and purchasing some apples, pears, plums, and a few bottles of drinking water, the four travelers loaded back into the old Buick Roadmaster and continued heading west.

About a hundred miles down the highway from the produce stand, the dusty dirty Buick pulled off the exit ramp onto Wagon Wheel Road.

The woman who had resumed her knitting, dropped it down on the seat and shouted, "Brian, what the hell are you doing?"

After stopping at the bottom of the exit ramp, the man turned to the woman and said, "Miss Paxton, if we don't get gas soon we'll have to start walking."

She said "Okay then you fool. Find a gas station and get back on the highway quickly and don't let the gas tank get that low again."

Following the signs with directions leading to the only general store and gas station in the area, Brian slowly drove avoiding large cracks and potholes in the road. Approximately four and a half miles from the highway, the driver pulled the big green Buick into a gas station that came straight out of the roaring twenties era.

The lone gas pump was of a style normally seen in old movies or in old car museums with the big glass top and a pump handle that had to be cranked to dispense the fuel. The building looked like something right out of a ghost town, with dirty windows, a wooden walkway, and front doors that looked like they hadn't been opened or closed in a long time. A sign hung over the doorway that read, "Rollie's General Store."

Though the old Buick had pulled up next to the pump, no one had come out of the building to pump the gas, so the driver went in through the old rickety looking doors.

Inside the store sitting next to the counter, a rather heavy man looked up from the small black and white TV he was watching and said, "Welcome to Rollie's, can I help you?"

"I need to get some gas. Does that old pump still work?"

"That one out there hasn't worked in many years mister, but out back there's a whole new pump and tank. If you drive around back, you can fill her up there."

Walking back out the same door he came in, the old man went down the steps and got back into the car. As he started the engine, the woman said, "Well, are you going to get gas or not?"

"We have to go around to the back Miss Paxton."

The back of the building was like the difference between night and day, with a modern gas pump, and loads of new lumber. There was a new cement foundation that looked freshly poured and it appeared to be for the new building extension.

After filling the Buick's gas tank and buying a few items in the store like a dozen candy bars and couple cans of soda, the man was on his way out of the door when he heard the old rotund man say, "Maybe by the next time through here mister, I'll have the place all fixed up."

Brian answered, "Thank you, but I don't think we'll be coming through here again. We're a long way from home."

About halfway back to the highway, one of the little girls in the back seat started crying, and the woman asked, "What are you crying for?"

Lisa Soto through her tears said, "I want to go home. I want my mommy."

"I'm your mommy now dear, so stop your crying."

The second little girl also started crying, and the woman asked, "Now what's your problem sweetheart?"

Hiding her face in her hands the second child said, "I want my mommy too, please take me home."

Miss Paxton smiled and said, "My little darlings, there is no need to cry. We are heading for our new home in a wonderful place with lots of trees, friendly animals and a beautiful lake where you can fish or swim anytime you like. Now put your heads down and get some sleep. It's going to be a long trip."

5

Three weeks had passed since the kidnapping of Lisa Soto, with only sparse information provided by the FBI in their investigation. Rosie was constantly on the phone trying to get assistance from many of the high-ranking officials she had met in her years with the police department.

The first week everyone wanted to come to her aide, with many of the high ranking officials offering to help in anyway possible. By the second week some still promised to help, but when Rosie made the phone calls for help she was palmed off on someone with lesser pull in the power department. By the third week, no one wanted to answer her calls for help any longer and if one happened to get through, she was told, "I'm sorry, but there's nothing we can do."

Dealing with the three weeks of despair, Rosie had turned to an old crutch for support. It seemed the only thing that could help her sleep at night was the whiskey bottle. During the years of her rehabilitation from the shooting incident, the slow process started a dependence on alcohol that Rosie began relying on daily to help chase away the feeling of self-pity.

Instead of the horrible kidnapping of Lisa bringing Rosie and her daughter Juanita closer, the constant drinking seemed to drive a wedge between them. An intervention arranged by an ex-partner and her Watch Commander from her early days on the Newark Police Department got Rosie to back away from the bottle and take a better look at her life.

Using her membership at the gym, Rosie planned to start a daily regimen of getting her body and mind into better condition than it had been in many years. At five feet seven, and one hundred and fifty pounds at the time of the shooting that ended her career, she was in top condition. Now looking into a mirror at the gym at two hundred and five pounds, she could hardly identify the one time officer who moved with grace. Rosie was once a strong woman who could defend herself against any opponent. With the skill she had learned in the many years of martial arts training, she was a fierce competitor to anyone who challenged her. Her workouts now at the gym were being done without her daughter's knowledge and she preferred to keep it that way. If what she had decided to do ended in failure, she didn't want to disappoint her daughter.

Rosie had made the decision to try to regain that self confidence she once had and start on that long road back. She knew it wouldn't be easy, but she was hatching a plan in her mind.

6

Waking up at 5 am on a Monday morning was not something Rosie had done in many years, not since her early days with the Newark Police Department. Lying in bed staring at the ceiling, the one time highly respected officer of the law thought about the past few years with disgust.

The feeling of failure had come over her, failure at her career, failure as a parent who was never there for her daughter, and now failure as a human being. The thought of changing her lifestyle including eating habits and daily exercises was the first step and she knew it, but getting her ass out of bed had to come first. Digging through her closet Rosie pulled out boxes that had been put away since her departure from the police force.

Halfway down into the first box she came across folded-up sets of jogging clothes that she was sure would not fit her any longer but decided to give it a shot. Taking off her nightgown and putting on a pair of panties, she then tried on the stretch pants of the jogging set. As she pulled and tugged them over enlarged parts of her extremities, she said aloud, "Holy shit."

She felt like she was trying to stuff a watermelon into a Glad sandwich bag, and looking into the mirror she had to laugh at herself a little, but inside felt the tears welling up.

Realizing that she had better toughen up a little before she put her plan in motion, she wiped her eyes and said loudly, "BULLSHIT."

It was the start of her plan that morning, one that she had been thinking seriously. She peeled off the pants, threw them into the trash can, and said to herself, "Enough of this shit."

In the second box that she opened, folded neatly, was a dress blue uniform, and under that in a leather case, a 38 Smith and Wesson revolver. After leaving the department, she always felt she would never have a need for a weapon again, but the new plans for her life would require her to obtain a permit to carry the weapon once again.

After dressing in some old loose fitting clothes, Rosie walked to the gym, a walk she had taken many times before, but this time she had a different agenda. When she walked in the front door she was greeted by the receptionist and the head trainer. The trainer was smiling, and in a very sarcastic voice he asked, "Are we ready for our daily workout Miss Castro?"

Rosie said, "Freddy, we need to have a little talk. Would you excuse us for a few minutes Barbara?"

Walking into the #1 training room, which was empty at that early hour, Rosie told the trainer, "Freddy, as of today, I will require your personal attention on getting my fat ass into top shape if you're up for the challenge. My plan is to lose about sixty pounds, and return to the shape I was in when I left the police force. I'm asking you. Are you up for the challenge? I will pay you extra for your personal attention. My plan is to work my ass off everyday until I feel like my old self."

Freddy smiled and said, "Miss Castro, if you're serious, I will help you in any way I can, but I would like to know what your new found drive is, so I can evaluate your commitment."

"Freddy, I know you've heard that my granddaughter was kidnapped about three weeks ago. Although the police and FBI are doing their best, now it's my turn to investigate, and please call me Rosie. I don't know what the future will bring but I do know that I refuse to just sit on my fat ass and do nothing."

He asked, "Are you saying you're going after the kidnappers?"

"Let's just say I'm getting seriously involved. So what do you say, will you be my trainer and help put me back in shape?"

Freddy held out his hand and said, "You got my help Rosie, when do we start?"

"We start today and then everyday if you're up to the challenge."

7

The New York Branch of the FBI worked diligently to locate Lisa Soto, notifying all the Agency's field offices around the country, supplying them with a complete description and photographs. In the beginning it was the number one case, and it seemed like the manpower being used could only result in the successful reuniting of the little girl with her family.

As time went on, the interest in the kidnapping didn't disappear, but the statistics involving child abductions points to the fact that as more and more time goes by, the odds on finding the child, get less and less.

Although the constant calls from Rosie and her daughter Juanita kept coming in checking on their progress, unfortunately they were told, "We are sorry to inform you, that there is no new news concerning Lisa Soto. We have been following all leads as they come in."

One agent, Tony Servantes, had a personal interest in the kidnapping because of a long time friendship with Rosie. The two met in third grade of grammar school in Newark, New Jersey. A very frail Rosalita Ricardo was being tormented by a bunch of white bread kids who were teasing her about her last name. They were calling her Ricky Ricardo, and wanted to know where Lucy was. Tony, a soft spoken kid himself, came to her rescue.

At first it was just harmless teasing, but when it turned to abusive language and pushing, Rosie broke down and her new friend jumped in to help her. Tony pushed one of the kids away from Rosie and put his arm around her, and the two of them walked home together. Living only one block away from each other, in the Puerto Rican neighborhood in Newark, the two kids became close friends.

Newark, New Jersey in the early days had a Puerto Rican neighborhood, White neighborhood, Black neighborhood and an Italian neighborhood. It wasn't right, but that's just how neighborhoods were divided. It took time and it was way overdue, but eventually those lines that separated neighborhoods disappeared and people just learned how to live together. All that had changed by the time Rosie moved away and she was glad to see it come about.

Rosie once said she heard an old black man say, "I'm going to live in whatever neighborhood I damn well please. If you don't like it, you can knock on my door and tell me, and I'll come out and put a bullet in your ass in my neighborhood."

Tony and Rosie became closer friends as they grew but never got romantically involved. They both looked at their relationship as more of a brother and sister type relationship, and that has lasted right up to present day.

Rosie had called Tony and asked him to meet her at a local diner, where she confided in him about her plans to try and find her granddaughter. He tried so hard to change her mind by telling her, "Just let the FBI handle everything."

She told him that she understands that the FBI is doing all they can do, but she cannot sit and wait any longer. Tony reached across the table in the booth they were sitting in, took her hand in his and said, "Rosie, you know how much I care for you, and I also know that you're a very competent smart woman, but this is a crazy thing you want to do."

Rosie smiled at him and said, "You're a wonderful man, a good friend who has always been there for me, but you got to understand, I'm doing this and I need your support."

"Sweetheart, of course I'll support you, but you're in no condition to be chasing kidnappers across country."

"Wait a minute, how do you know they went cross country? Tony, what else do you know?"

"Not enough for you to go on a wild goose chase."

"Tell me Tony, what the hell are you keeping from me, I need your help"

"Rosie, I could get in a shit load of trouble if they find out that I have revealed any information to you."

"Stop the bullshitting Tony, and tell me."

"I pulled the file on your granddaughter's kidnapping yesterday. The first confirmed sighting was in eastern Pennsylvania at a roadside fruit and vegetable stand. There were two adults, a woman around fifty to sixty, and a man around sixty, accompanied by two little girls."

"Wait a minute, two little girls?"

"Yes, there's no report about the second child yet."

"How long ago was this?"

"Nine days following the report of the disappearance of your granddaughter."

"That was three weeks ago?"

"Yes, your granddaughter was positively identified from the photographs your daughter supplied the department with."

"What town was that in?"

"A place called Lehighton, about twenty miles north of Allentown, on Interstate Route 476."

"You said there were two little girls?"

"Yes, both about the same age."

"Are there any other leads?"

"They were next spotted in a little town off Interstate 80, still in Pennsylvania, at a gas station and general store. A small spot on the map called Rosecrans, about twenty five miles west of Lewisburg."

"Tony, why did you keep this from me? Why didn't you tell me three weeks ago?"

"Rosie, I didn't know it three weeks ago, it was an investigation, and it's still an investigation. I shouldn't be telling you this now."

"You're my friend, my best friend, and you would keep this from me?"

"Rosie, if I thought we could go and find your granddaughter right now, I would drive you there, where-ever there is, please believe me."

"Tony, it's something I got to do. I'm not ready yet, but I will be soon."

"Don't do it Rosie, leave it to the Bureau, they may be slow, but they know what they're doing, please think this out."

Getting up from the table, the two old friends hugged, and Rosie said, "Tony, you'll always be my best friend and I trust you with my life. I promise you, I will stay in touch with you. Please, please call me on my cell if you get anymore information on Lisa."

"I'm going to keep working on you to change your mind Rosie, but if I can't, I'll do anything I can to help."

Rosie kissed him on the cheek, and then walked home.

8

It had been a little over five weeks since Rosie had started seriously working out at the gym, and with the help of Freddy, she had managed to lose over thirty pounds, and was in the best shape she had been in, in a long time. Applying for a Private Investigator's License and a permit to carry a concealed weapon took a little bit of manipulation, and a few well placed phone calls, but she pulled it off. Her license and permit were temporary and only good in her state, but at least she had some documentation that could possibly get her out of a jam if stopped in another state where possessing a weapon was restricted.

Rosie knew she would have to purchase a vehicle that would be practical for her needs. Her decision was to purchase a camper van, where she could sleep and cook her meals. The money she would use came from the insurance settlement she received years ago from her husband's death.

Although the money received from the insurance company was put into a special savings account for Lisa's college education, this was a special emergency, and it would now be used. But she had to change her plans a little when Juanita told her, "Mom, I'm going with you."

This was not acceptable to Rosie, but her unstable and very emotional daughter broke down crying and going into a rage when she was told no.

Rosie told her, "Sweetheart, this is not going to be easy and I need to know that you are safe at home."

Juanita told her mom how her life meant nothing any longer without Lisa, and if she went on the search without her, she could not survive the worrying time alone. Reluctantly following a very long discussion, Rosie agreed to take her daughter with her, but certain guide lines were set.

It would be a couple more weeks before the two women could start on their quest, and there were many things that had to be taken care of first.

All of Rosie's belongings would be put in storage, with the exception of her pet parakeet that a neighbor agreed to care for, and her apartment would be given up. She told Juanita, "I always hated that apartment. When we return with Lisa, we will all live together in a big house."

The rent on Juanita's apartment would automatically be paid from a special account set up by Rosie. After weighing the options, it was decided that Juanita's dog, a small forty pound Lab named Sandy, would travel with them, providing added security for the two searchers.

Juanita agreed to attend workout sessions with her mom to get herself in better physical condition, and she would accompany Rosie to the Staten Island Firing Range for instruction on the proper use of a firearm.

Tony Servantes was staying in constant contact with Rosie and trying over and over to talk her out of what he felt was a very dangerous trip that was now imminent. Although Tony was completely against Rosie's plans, he did supply her with any information on the elderly couple that abducted her granddaughter and the direction they appeared to be heading.

With so much time passing since the confirmed sighting of her granddaughter and the kidnappers in Pennsylvania, Rosie knew it was time to get on the road. Juanita, after only two weeks of very strenuous workouts, and constant instructions on proper investigative procedures, was a little better prepared for the road ahead.

The instructions and actual firing of a weapon at the firing range appeared to be useless because of Juanita's fear of guns. It had been part of the agreement she had made with Rosie so she was keeping her word no matter how much she hated doing it.

On a Tuesday morning, Rosie and Juanita sat in the twenty-eight foot motor-coach van that Rosie had purchased. It was loaded for the trip with supplies, and even Sandy the dog looked anxious to get on the way. Rosie told her daughter, "Look around dear, we may not be back here for a long time."

As they started to pull away from the curb, her dear friend Tony pulled his car on an angle in front of the van. He got out of the car to try one last time to convince Rosie that this whole idea was crazy and should be abandoned.

Standing next to her open driver's window, Tony said, "Rosie Sweetheart, don't do this, we will find your granddaughter and bring her home to you."

"Tony, I know you mean what you say, but so do I. Now please, move your car or I'll push it out of my way, *Sweetheart*."

9

Leaving Brooklyn, driving across the Verrazano Narrows Bridge into Staten Island, Rosie and Juanita listened to the traffic reports for awhile then talked about happier days when Juanita was a little girl, and Rosie was a rookie on the police force. Tears came to Juanita's eyes when she thought of her father and the wonderful years they spent together.

Rosie spoke of her late husband with much fondness and told her daughter how she had loved him very much, and always would. Juanita and her dad were very close and it was just a miracle that she was not with him on that horrible day when he was shot and killed at the bank.

As they approached the Goethals Bridge, that would take them to New Jersey, Rosie suggested that it would be a good idea if they stopped for breakfast in a little while.

After driving approximately ten miles since crossing the bridge to New Jersey, Rosie pulled into a parking lot of a truck stop with a diner in a town called Union. They parked right in front under a big shade tree so they could keep an eye on their vehicle as they ate. The dog Sandy sat in the driver's seat watching the two women enter the diner, and would remain there until they returned an hour later.

While in the diner, sitting at a booth by one of the front windows, Rosie and Juanita were approached by one of the local wanna-be Casanovas. The burly jerk asked them, "What are two beauties like you doing at a truck stop this early in the morning? Are you scouting for early morning dates?"

Over the years growing up around many men of this type, and without missing a beat, Rosie answered, "We were just discussing where the closest venereal disease clinic might be, so maybe you can help us?"

The stranger quickly retreated back to his seat at the counter giving Rosie the one finger salute as he backed away.

Juanita asked her mother, "How could you say such a thing? What must that man think of us?"

Rosie smiled and said, "Dear, do you really care what that piece of slime thinks? He's only thinking of one thing, and it's not our welfare. I know it won't be easy for you, but you're going to have to develop a kind of hard shell around yourself."

"But he didn't seem that bad."

"Sweetheart, his tongue was hanging on the floor when we walked in earlier. And when I passed his table on my way to the ladies room before, he made a remark to his friend about my ass."

"Mom, how long do you think we will be away from home?"

"Honey, I wish I had an answer for you. We can only take this one-day at a time, and go where the clues take us. With any luck we'll catch up to those bastards sooner than later, but one thing for sure, we're going to find them."

10

Not forgetting to bring out a small treat for their loyal watchdog Sandy, Rosie un-wrapped a napkin containing two strips of bacon. Jumping up with anticipation, it had the tan Lab falling all over herself trying to please in anyway possible.

Sitting in the motor home Rosie told Juanita, "This may be your last chance to change your mind about coming along with me. Please sweetheart, think carefully about the dangers involved."

"Mom, start the engine and let's get going, we have a long trip ahead of us."

Rosie hugged her daughter and said, "Okay, you're the navigator, start navigating."

Juanita opened her large map book containing highly detailed state maps and looked at the highlighted route that Rosie had carefully plotted. "You already did most of the work mom."

Starting the engine and pulling out of the parking lot onto the highway, Rosie said, "On paper it looks easy, but you'll have to let me know when we are getting close to a turn-off and which way we have to go."

Rosie knew the first confirmed sighting of the kidnappers was approximately eighty miles west in Pennsylvania, in a town called Lehighton, on highway I-476, and she figured it would take about an hour and a half to two hours to get there as long as they didn't run into much traffic.

With only having two confirmed locations where the kidnappers were spotted, both in Pennsylvania, Rosie knew she would have to be very careful with her choices of direction to follow afterward.

The old route, Route 22 in New Jersey, had merged with Interstate I-78. The new road was not as scenic as the old road, but it was much more efficient. With light traffic and good weather they crossed into Pennsylvania in shorter time than expected.

Continuing on I-78 into Allentown, the women made the transition to the new highway and headed north on I-476 to Lehighton.

Following directions supplied by Tony, Rosie found the fruit and vegetable stand considerably easy, with only having to back-track a mile after passing it, thinking it was a deserted building.

Driving with the windows open, they were enjoying the wonderful fresh air that had a quality that made Rosie and Juanita long for a better way of life than the city they had been living in for so long. Rosie slowly pulled off the highway and looked for a place to park.

Although the large wooden shutters were closed down and the building did look like it hadn't been used in years, it became obvious to Rosie that it was only a temporary shut down for repairs once she read a hand painted sign.

Parking the camper at the side of the building, the two women and Sandy got out to stretch their legs and for Sandy to find a suitable location to relieve herself. While standing in front of the boarded up building, discussing what their next move would be, an elderly woman approached them from the side of the stand and said, "Sorry ladies, but we're closed for remodeling."

Rosie spoke up and said, "Thank you, but we're looking for Hilda Brunson, the proprietor of this stand."

"Well young lady, you found her, I'm Hilda, and this is my stand."

Hilda Brunson looked much older than her years, somewhere around seventy Rosie guessed. Her sun-drenched skin was very tan and wrinkled from obvious over exposure to the sun. She stood around 5'10" and was around 150 lbs, with gray hair pulled back in a pony tail. Her bright blue eyes sparkled when she smiled, and it was easy to see that she must have been a real beauty when she was younger not to take away from her looks now, because she still remains a very attractive senior.

Rosie extended her hand and introduced herself and Juanita. She then asked the woman if they could have a few minutes of her time.

After only a couple of minutes of explaining what their mission was, Hilda interrupted her and said, "Dear let's go into the house. I'll put on a pot of coffee or if you'd like, some lemonade, and I'll try to help you as much as I can."

Juanita said, "What about Sandy mom?"

Hilda asked, "Sandy, who's Sandy?"

"She's our dog."

"Oh she'll be fine. With all the animals around here, the smells will keep her busy for hours."

Walking up the road behind the stand toward a farmhouse that looked like it had been built a hundred years earlier, Rosie asked, "If you don't mind me asking Hilda, how long have you lived here?"

Hilda laughed and said, "All my life dear. I was born in the bedroom of the house that stood where the vegetable stand now sits, seventy two years ago."

Looking around, Juanita remarked, "I envy you Hilda, I would love to live in surroundings like this, where children can grow up and not fear the dangers of the city."

"Oh at times it's been a challenge dear, with all the work that needs to be done each day, life just seems to pass you by."

Juanita just seemed to stare off into space and the tears started streaming down her face. Rosie quickly hugged her and said, "We'll find her Sweetheart, we'll find her."

11

Stepping up onto the front porch of the weather worn farmhouse may have brought scowls and sneers from most city dwellers, but to Rosie it was different. Though the wooden porch was in need of paint and repairs, a warm comfortable looking swing, with fluffy pillows seemed to beckon anyone to rest and enjoy themselves.

A card table with two chairs sat at the other end of the porch with a partially completed puzzle pushed to one side. A few steps from the door sat a rocking chair with an old orange crate used to hold magazines.

As Hilda opened the screen door, she called out, "Frank, we have company, now you put on a shirt dear."

Walking into the house, the aroma of a freshly baked pie was overwhelming, and instantly brought a smile to Juanita's face as she said, "Oh my, something smells so good in here."

An elderly man about seventy-five responded, "Oh that's just my new aftershave young lady. I use it to try and cover up that other smell of something Hilda threw together in the kitchen."

While they all broke out laughing, Hilda introduced her husband to the two women. She said, "Frank, these two young ladies need our help with some information. Now please dear, go put on a shirt, and I'll put on some coffee and if you behave yourself you can have a slice of pie."

The interior of the old farmhouse was not what one would expect walking through the front door. The hardwood floor from the front door to the kitchen had been worn from constant foot traffic, but the rest of the living room was spotless, with carpeting, drapes, and very expensive looking furniture.

The walls were painted in a forest green and the beautiful woodwork was highly polished, and in the far right corner surrounded by tasteful artwork, stood a baby grand piano. The entire room was light and cheery, not what was expected at all. Walking into the dining room, the sun shining in through the French doors leading to the back porch brought an "Oh my, from Rosie's mouth."

In the center of the room was a table that could obviously seat twelve if so needed, and against the far wall a wet bar and a well-stocked liquor cabinet. A china cabinet and a beautiful grandfather clock were the only other furnishings in the room.

Following Hilda into the kitchen, Rosie and Juanita were again surprised to see a full chef's kitchen, fit for and supplied with enough cooking utensils to keep a gourmet chef in his glory.

Rosie felt she had to say something, so holding her hands out, palms up, she said, "Hilda, you have a beautiful home, one that you can be so proud of."

"Dear, I only wish I had more family around to enjoy it with Frank and me. The kids have all grown and moved away, and they only come to visit on some holidays. It's the only time when this old house is truly alive, and me too."

Juanita stood by the kitchen island and said, "Ma'am, I would never leave this house, not for any city in the world. Your home looks like it would fit in with any of the beautiful homes they put in those fancy magazines."

"Well, before we talk about anything else, I want you both to know that you are welcome back here any time. Now let me put on the coffee and then you can tell me all about your plans and your granddaughter."

Rosie and Juanita sat on the stools at the island counter and watched as Hilda moved around the kitchen so gracefully. As she moved she hummed a sweet song un-familiar to the women.

Juanita asked, "What is the name of that song you're humming?"

"Oh its just something I wrote many years ago dear. I always enjoyed making up songs when I was a child, it's a part of me that I never grew out of."

12

After explaining to Hilda all that led up to the present day, both Rosie and Juanita appeared to be emotionally spent. Hilda's husband Frank, who had been standing by the doorway to the kitchen, spoke up and said, "When the FBI came here to question us five weeks ago, I told them about a couple who had two small children with them, and the reason I remembered them was the car the man was driving."

Rosie had her notebook out as she asked, "What kind of car was it Frank?"

"I had one just like it many years ago. It was a 1968 Buick Roadmaster, Rosie. They don't make em like that anymore."

"What color was it Frank?"

"Two-tone green, a light pastel green roof and a forest green body, she was a beauty."

"Did you notice anything else about the car, dents, whitewall tires, anything at all?"

"It had a big antenna bolted on the rear bumper, you know, the kind used for a CB radio. They're not used anymore, and I thought it looked like crap on such a classic car."

"What did the kids look like Frank?"

"Hilda, you got a better look at the kids than I did."

"They were both young," Hilda said. "I would guess around seven, or eight, not older."

"Do you remember what they were wearing, jeans or a dress?"

"No I'm sorry dear I don't. The one child may have had on a yellow sweater, but I'm not sure."

Juanita held her hand up to her mouth and said, "Oh my god that was Lisa. She was wearing a yellow sweater. I made her put it on before I would let her go outside."

As Frank left the room he said, "Excuse me, I'll be right back."

Hearing a scratching sound, Hilda walked to the back door of the kitchen and opened it slowly. Sitting there with her head cocked to one side, and her tongue hanging down a little, Sandy was wagging her tail brushing the porch floor.

Bending down a little and petting Sandy's head, Hilda said, "I'm sorry sweetheart let me get you some water."

Sandy, not waiting for an invitation, ran through the open screen door to Rosie's side and sat down.

Rosie said, "I'm sorry Hilda, I'll put her back outside."

"It's alright dear this kitchen has seen many pets."

As Hilda filled a bowl with water, she told Rosie that everything she had told her so far was in the report to the FBI, but there was one other thing she remembered.

"The woman, who I think was in her fifties, walked with a severe limp, and I think she had a prosthetic leg, the right one."

Juanita asked, "A what kind of leg?"

Rosie said, "An artificial leg."

"You mean like a wooden leg?"

"Wood or metal could even be plastic over metal. She may have lost her leg because of diabetes."

Frank came back into the room carrying a photo album, placed it on the table and said, "Here's the kind of car you're looking for."

Looking at a picture Frank was pointing at in the album, Rosie asked, "Can you spare one of these pictures by any chance?"

"I can do better then that, follow me."

Walking to a room off of the dining room, Frank turned on the computer and the printer, and after only a few minutes, Rosie had a blown up color picture of the Buick Roadmaster.

Rosie asked, "How did you do that, your car was a different color?"

"It's amazing what these new printers can do dear."

Although Rosie had a copy of the FBI report with the descriptions of the man and woman, she wrote down all of the details Hilda and Frank provided.

Rosie looked at Juanita and said, "It's time for us to get back on the road sweetheart."

Thanking the wonderfully warm couple for all their hospitality and help, they knew they had stayed too long but all the information they had gathered was well worth the time.

Hilda had put together a large bag of fruit, and placed one of her freshly baked apple pies in a Tupperware container made for pies. Holding a cardboard box in her hands she said, "And here are a few things for Sandy to chew on during your trip."

Looking into the box Rosie saw chew toys and a box of dog biscuits and said, "Thank you Hilda for your kind gifts, I'm sure they'll give Sandy many hours of fun. And as for the pie, I can't wait to stick a fork in it to taste the fresh apples."

Rosie asked Frank about the next town they had to locate and if he had ever heard about it. She said, "Any information about the town of Rosecrans would be very helpful."

Frank said, "I went through Rosecrans a few years back but I don't really recall much about it. I can give you the info on which highways will get you there, but that's about it."

Walking out to the camper, Frank gave Rosie directions to I-80 which would take her to the area of the general store and gas station.

With hugs all around, Hilda said, "Stay safe girls, and please hurry back soon. You're always welcome anytime."

Rosie told her, "Thank you both so much, you have been a big help and I promise I will let you know how things turn out. I wrote down your phone number, so I will call also."

Hilda smiled and said, "Dear I'm way ahead of you. When you open the pie container you'll find our names, address, and phone number. May God direct and protect you both."

13

As Rosie started to drive away from the fruit and veggie stand, she saw Hilda waving her arms in the air signaling her to stop. Walking up to the driver's side of the RV, Hilda told Rosie, "Frank just told me the old Buick had Illinois plates. That may tell you where they're headed."

"Thank you Hilda, that is a big help. Please thank Frank also."

Once again they started to pull out on the highway but had to wait for a few cars and an eighteen wheeler to go by. Safely on the pavement and picking up speed, Rosie said, "It's sure nice to know that there are people in this world like Hilda and Frank. I know we have some good neighbors at home, but they're kind of special."

Driving down the road only a few miles, Rosie pulled the RV off to the side in a small clearing.

Juanita, who had been studying the map at the table asked, "What's up mom?"

"I decided to give Tony a call and let him know about the car they were driving, year, make, color, and license plates, just in case he doesn't know."

On the third ring, Agent Servantes noticed the caller ID and answered, "Well it's about time I heard from you."

Rosie said with a slight laugh, "You damn fool; we've only been gone a few hours. Are you going to tell me you miss us already?"

"So you called to tell me you're turning back, right?"

"Hell no Tony. I just wanted to tell you how nice it is out here in the country. We met a couple of the nicest people on this planet."

He asked, "So where are you?"

"We're in Leighton. Look, I got more info on the car the kidnappers were driving."

"Yeah I know it was an old green Buick."

"To be exact, it was a 1968 Buick Roadmaster two-tone green with Illinois license plates. And one other thing, it had one of those big CB whip antennas on the rear bumper"

"You know, that makes sense. The Cleveland, Ohio branch office of the Bureau came up with something. They believe the vehicle was spotted at a Howard Johnson's. They said a couple with children fitting the description spent two nights at the motel."

"So they were spotted in Cleveland?"

"Actually it was about twenty miles southwest of Cleveland just off I-80, on the Ohio Turnpike, in Elyria."

"Are they sure it was them?"

"They brought attention to themselves because the woman and one of the two children with them had come down with a case of severe chest congestion. From what we've been able to find out, they both had dangerously high temperatures also. They needed to visit the Emergency Room at the local hospital and several of the hospital staff remembered them."

Rosie said, "Elyria huh?"

"They couldn't provide proper identification and paid in cash when questioned by admitting."

"Did they get a good description?"

Tony said, "Better than that, they got a picture of the happy couple and both kids on the hospital security camera."

Rosie asked, "And?"

"Yes it *was* Lisa with them, along with a child named Elizabeth Schorr, who was also kidnapped from her schoolyard in Queens, New York. The Schorr family had reported it three months ago, but the two kidnappings were never linked together until just recently"

Rosie put her phone down for a few seconds. "Oh my God, those bastards are sick."

"What mom?" Juanita asked.

Rosie picked her phone back up, "Sorry Tony. That just caught me off guard. Go on."

"The parents of the other child have been notified and the investigation has resumed with the additional information on Lisa also."

"You mean that they had stopped looking for that little girl and my granddaughter?"

"No Rosie, they have not stopped looking for Lisa or the other girl. Now it has become a joint investigation involving both children and clues from the Schorr kidnapping are being reviewed with new interest."

"Is there anything new that can help me catch up to them?"

"Because an intern at the hospital admired the old Buick in the parking lot, and an agent in Cleveland kept asking questions on his own time, we have some new leads in the case. So you can turn that home on wheels around and head back and leave the investigating to the professionals."

Rosie said, "Thank you Tony, but no way. We're not turning around and that's final."

"Rosie, please."

"Tony, we are not coming back home until Lisa is safe in her mother's arms."

Tony pleaded, "But Rosie."

"Oh by the way, did you know that the woman has a prosthetic leg?"

"No, how did you find out that information?"

"It's called police work Tony. I'll call you in a few days sweetheart. Bye."

Tony said, "Rosie wait," But it was too late; the phone went dead.

14

By the time Rosie and Juanita reached the town of
Rosecrans, the big golden ball in the sky was just
touching the mountain peaks to the west. With a
little directional help from one of the locals, they
were soon pulling into the parking lot in front of
Rollie's General Store and Gas Station. The sun
was setting fast and they knew it was time to start
looking for a place to spend the night.

Rosie spotted a big shade tree to park under,
figuring if they spent the night it would help keep
the motor home from getting too hot in the
morning sun.

After locking the motor home they followed
the signs and arrows pointing the way to the new
entrance for the store. The women walked on the

temporary walkway made of plywood around to the rear of the building.

An elderly gentleman, probably in his sixties, overweight, red faced, holding a pipe in one hand and a tobacco pouch in the other, sat in a chair next to the newly constructed doorway to the store. As the man turned his head he smiled and said, "Welcome to Rollie's, can I help you?"

Also smiling, Rosie asked, "Would you be Mr. Rollie by any chance?"

"Just Rollie dear, I wouldn't know how to act if people started calling me mister. What can I do for you?"

"Mind if I sit and ask you a few questions?"

"As long as you don't get too personal, I would enjoy the company and the conversation."

"My name is Rosie Castro and this is my daughter Juanita Soto. We are trying to find my granddaughter who was kidnapped from New York about two months ago."

"Excuse me for interrupting dear, but the FBI has been here twice asking questions about the kidnappers and I told them everything that I could remember."

"Thank you Rollie, I really appreciate all your help, but their investigation has stalled. My being an ex-police detective, I've decided to follow up and try to track them down."

"You sure don't look like a detective ma'am."

"I'm hoping that works in our favor Rollie."

"So what can I help you with Rosie?"

"We know the car they were driving was an old Buick. It was two toned green with Illinois license plates, and that's probably where they're headed. Was there anything you may have overheard that might give us more information on the kidnappers?"

"The man paid cash for the items he purchased, and his gas and oil."

"What items did he buy?"

Rollie thought a few seconds and said "He bought a few bottles of water, a couple of bags of potato chips, a bunch of candy bars, and a couple of maps if I remember right."

"Do you remember by chance which maps he bought Rollie?"

"I remembered that one of them was Ohio, but I couldn't remember the other one. My wife pointed out that we had a few empty spaces in the map rack on the wall last week. It got me to thinking more about it. I remember selling two maps to Joe Curtis from Curtis Hardware. He took the Florida and Georgia ones, but neither I nor my wife could remember selling the Nevada map to anyone. So it's possible that was the other map he bought."

Rosie said, "Nevada huh?"

"Yeah that desert place out west, hot as hell and nothing grows there but cactus and sand."

Rosie smiled and said, "I've never been there myself Rollie, but I heard it's not that bad a place to live."

"Yeah, we don't usually sell too many maps, most people around here know where they're going, and they sure don't need a map to get there."

"Can you think of anything else that might help us?"

"Rosie I sure can't, and like I told that agent, if I remember something else, I'll call them."

"Rollie, if I could bother you for one more thing. Is there a place around here where we can park for the night?"

"Rosie, that's a nice place right over there where you're parked by that oak tree, and it looks like it has your name on it for the night."

"Thank you Rollie you're a dear, I'd be happy to pay you something for the parking, and we do need to gas up."

"Don't worry about the parking, and when you're ready, the pumps are always on, just help yourself and let me or my wife know how much you got."

"Thank you Rollie, you have been a big help, and a real gentleman."

Rollie sat up tall and said, "Oh something else Rosie. We serve breakfast here on the porch from 5 to 10AM if you're an early riser. There's a menu on the wall right behind you with some of the specials."

"I didn't realize you had a diner her too."

"The little building at the end of the porch is a kitchen, and my wife Brenda loves to cook."

"So its just breakfast served?"

"Yup, maybe someday we'll do lunch and dinner, but for now it's just a hearty country breakfast."

"Oh Rollie, do you remember what kind of candy bars the kidnapper bought?"

"They were Mounds dear. I remember because there were only six left in the box on the counter and he asked me if I had anymore."

"He got them for the kids I guess?" Rosie said.

"No, I would guess they were for him. I know because he ate one before he left the store, and put the others in his pockets."

"Mounds, very good Rollie, the old man liked Mounds candy bars."

"Watch that old man stuff now Rosie, he was closer to my age than I want to admit."

"You still look pretty young to me Rollie."

He smiled and said, "I think I'll go and kiss my wife and tell her what you said."

"Night Rollie, and thanks again."

15

Rosie, Juanita, and Sandy walked around looking at the surrounding fields of farmland as dusk was settling in on them. A few animals here and there but mostly it was a calm and quiet environment. The air smelled so fresh even with the occasional whiff of cow and steer manure.

Sandy was enjoying the freedom of walking and sniffing along the fence line at all the new scents, and relieving herself wherever she saw fit.

Walking slowly back to the motor home, Rosie put her arm around Juanita and told her, "Dear, we need to get an early start in the morning. The town of Elyria in Ohio is about five-hundred miles away and we'll spend most of the day getting there, so let's get to bed quickly and be rested for the long drive in the morning."

The kind of sleep Rosie experienced that night was the type we all have had at one time or another. She had just put her head down on the pillow, closed her eyes, reopened them and it was morning. Although she had expected to toss and turn all night, it didn't happen and she was glad. This type of sleep does not leave a person well rested and in most cases not very alert but she was ready to go.

After waking Juanita, the two women got themselves ready for the day ahead, and after enjoying a wonderful country breakfast at Brenda's Kitchen Diner, said goodbye to Rollie and his wife.

The day started out as a beautiful dry sunny day, but by the time they traveled only one hundred miles, the women found themselves in some of the worst weather they had ever seen. The rain came down not just in buckets but in monsoon type rainfall.

Just outside of a town called Falls Creek, Pennsylvania on Highway 80, the motor home experienced engine problems and stopped running. The dead vehicle left the women stranded in a dense forest like area on the shoulder of the road with the heavy rain pounding on the roof.

After making a few calls on her cell phone, Rosie found out that the closest repair facility that would work on her motor home was in the city of DuBois about five miles away.

A very friendly and overly talkative tow truck driver showed up in less than an hour, and after hooking up the vehicle started on the way to his repair shop in DuBois. As he drove he asked the women many questions about who they were and where they were going.

At first, maybe because of her harsh upbringing or maybe because of her police training, she told the driver he asked too many damn questions. When the driver seemed to push a little harder, Rosie told him it was really none of his business. The driver apologized and they continued in silence for awhile. By the time they reached the shop, Rosie's icy personality melted some and she opened up a little.

Actually she saw that the driver was a very nice person at heart, and was just a big friendly teddy bear that liked people and loved to ask questions.

Sitting in some heavy traffic and waiting for the congestion to clear, Rosie told the driver about the old couple and the kidnapping of her granddaughter. She told him about the fruit and vegetable stand, Rollie's General Store and the old' 68 Buick they were traveling in.

The seven-mile drive back to the shop took about forty-five minutes because of the weather and the stop-and-go traffic.

After a complete diagnosis of the motor home, it was determined that the cause of the malfunction was a defective electric fuel pump in the gas tank. Unfortunately the pump would not be available until the following day because no local suppliers carried that model in stock. The closest parts warehouse that had the pump in stock was in Clarion, which was located about thirty miles away. Their delivery truck only made one stop in DuBois daily and it had come and gone hours earlier.

The motor home, being parked next to the repair shop and not inside the building, allowed the women the option of spending the night in the vehicle. The shop owner gave his permission to do so, or they could stay at a motel a few blocks away and maybe be a little more comfortable for the night.

The women chose to stay with their belongings in the vehicle and it turned out to be a wise decision on their part. Somewhere around 8pm that night, there was a knock on the motor home door.

Looking out the window Rosie saw one of the mechanics who worked in the repair shop and she asked him, "Yes, who's there?"

The guy answered, "Miss Castro, my name is Robert and I work for Henry's Auto Repair. Can I talk with you for a few minutes?"

Rosie said, "Sure Robert, I'll be with you in a couple minutes."

Not being one to take chances, Rosie walked to the kitchen cabinet and retrieved her 38 Smith & Wesson, placing it next to her as she sat on the couch covering it with her jacket.

Motioning for Juanita to open the door, she listened as the young man walked in saying, "I hope I'm not bothering you ladies, but I think I have some information you can use."

Juanita said, "Have a seat Robert."

As the man sat at the small kitchenette table, he started talking about his friend who owned a repair shop in Grove City, about eighty miles west on I-80. Before he could say another word, Juanita asked, "Robert, can I get you something to drink, maybe a Coke or a beer?"

"No thank you ma'am, I don't drink beer, and Coke is too sweet, but maybe a bottle of water if you have one."

While Juanita got a couple bottles of water out of the refrigerator, Rosie asked, "Okay Robert, just what information do you have you think we could use?"

"My friend Steve called me three weeks ago and asked me if I knew where I could find a rear end differential for a 1968 Buick Roadmaster."

Leaning forward in her seat, Rosie asked, "Wait a minute Robert, who was it that called?"

"It was my friend Steve ma'am. He said he needed a rear for an old Buick that was sitting in his shop. He said it was a beautiful green Roadmaster that was in great shape but the rear end had burned up because of no gear oil. Jack, the tow truck driver told me you were looking for someone in an old green Buick Roadmaster and we don't see many of those around here."

"Robert, how long ago was this that your friend Steve called you?"

"It was about three weeks ago Miss Castro."

"And what was the name of the town he worked in?"

Robert clasped his hands in front of him on the table and said, "The town is called Grove City, ma'am."

"Robert. Please, stop calling me Miss Castro or ma'am, honest. Rosie's fine."

Juanita asked, "Were there children with them?"

"That I don't know ma'am, he only told me about the car, nothing about the people."

"How far is it from here?"

"About eighty miles Miss, ah, Rosie."

"What time tomorrow do you think we'll be back on the road Robert?"

"I think you should be back on the road by noon if the truck gets here early."

"Would you give us the full name of your friend and the shop he works at in Grove City and maybe some directions would be a great help?"

"Sure Miss Rosie."

Robert supplied Rosie with his friend's name and the shop name and address in Grove City. Rosie tried to give Robert a twenty dollar bill but he refused saying, "I hope you find your granddaughter Miss Rosie."

That next morning as the mechanic worked on the motor home, Rosie and Juanita went to a popular breakfast place in town that Robert recommended and had a bite to eat and some great coffee. By 11AM they were ready to continue on their journey west. With directions and the address of Robert's friend, Rosie had a good feeling the day would be rewarding.

16

The drive to Grove City took less than two hours with a light rain that was a continuation from the days before. Steve Ashton, the owner of Steve's Auto Service, had only one mechanic, an old burly guy named Gridley. The old wrench turner and oil service technician, as he liked to be called, looked very much like Fred Sanford, from the old TV show Sanford and Son. That "Redd Foxx" look, quick wit and his mechanical ability was a big reason why people just fell in love with the old guy. He was like the grandpa or great uncle that everyone wished they had.

When Rosie and Juanita pulled up to the gas pumps at Steve's shop, before she had a chance to turn off the motor, a tall blond haired man about forty approached the vehicle and welcomed the women to Grove City. Rosie could tell the person in front of her was Steve, by the nametag on his uniform.

Wasting no time Rosie held out her hand through the open window and said, "Hi Steve, my name is Rosie Castro, and this is my daughter Juanita. Did Robert from DuBois call you on our behalf?"

"Hi Rosie, yes he did, and what can I do to help you?"

"Well it's a long story, but we're trying to track down some people who came through here a few weeks ago and from what Robert told us, you may have done some work on their car."

"Yes, Robert told me it was that old Buick Roadmaster, a real beauty."

"Do you remember anything about the driver or the passengers?"

"The guy pulled up to the pumps, right where you're parked, with smoke pouring out from under the back of the vehicle and asked me to check it out."

"Did you notice any kids in the car?"

"Not at first, but when Gridley offered to drive them to the motel, (oh, he's my mechanic) that was when I saw the two kids in the back seat. I guess they were both about the same age, two girls, one had to be carried and the other walked on her own."

Juanita was frantic, as she kept asking, "Which one of the children was ill? What did she look like? Please, can you try to remember?"

"I'm sorry ma'am, I didn't pay much attention to the kids, but I can tell you this, the little girl the man carried to Gridley's car didn't look too good, I think she was unconscious."

Rosie asked, "Is your mechanic still around?"

A voice behind Rosie said, "I sure am little lady, what can I do for you?"

Rosie asked, "Gridley, what can you tell me about the people from that old Buick?"

"Well little lady."

"Please Gridley, call me Rosie."

"Well Rosie. The guy driving the car was I guess in his sixties. He was as tall as Steve, maybe six two around two hundred and forty pounds. I don't remember his eyes but he had gray hair. The woman was a mean lady son of a gun, maybe in her fifties or early sixties. She was maybe your height and around one hundred eighty or one hundred ninety pounds. Her hair was mostly gray with some light brown in it. She kind of looked like one of those Golden Girls on TV, the tall one with gray hair, but heavier.

"What about the kids, Gridley?"

"One of the little darlins was real sick Rosie, I could see that. I asked the man if I could take them to the hospital, but he told me she was fine. I told him it would be no trouble at all to go to the hospital on the way to the motel. The man got very aggravated and then he told me to mind my own business."

"Just one more question Gridley. Where did you drop them off?"

"I dropped them off at the Howard Johnson's down the road. It's a family friendly place with clean rooms and good food."

Juanita franticly asked, "Which child was it that was sick?"

"Well ma'am, it was the little girl with the red hair who was unconscious."

Juanita started to cry, then Rosie went to her side and hugged her, "We'll find her dear, we'll find her."

Rosie said, "Thank you very much Gridley for your help."

Gridley said, "I hope you find them ma'am."

Rosie asked Steve lots of questions and he provided her with a full description of the man and woman. He wrote out the license plate number, and best of all, a photostat copy of the man's driver's license. It was a New York license, but it was a photo ID with a clear picture.

For the first time there was a face and a name to go with the rotten crime committed by these horrible people. Rosie knew she had to get in touch with Tony and send him the picture and name of one of the kidnappers.

Returning to the motor home, Rosie retrieved her cell phone only to find out that her battery was dead. When she plugged it in to recharge, she found that she had three missed calls, all from Tony.

Allowing the phone only a few minutes to recharge, the first call she made was Tony. On the second ring he answered and said, "Where the hell have you been?"

"Tony, I have information for you."

"Well I have information for you too."

"Tony, I have the name and photo of one of the kidnappers. The man's name is Brian Doyle."

"How the hell did you get that?"

"It's a long story, but I need to get it to you."

"Rosie, where are you?"

"I'm in a town called Grove City, in Pennsylvania, about thirty or forty miles east of Youngstown Ohio."

"Hold on for a minute and let me check something."

"What do you mean hold on?"

"Just wait a minute. There's a branch office of the FBI in Youngstown, go in and talk to Agent

Richards, and have him call me when you get there."

"Ok, we'll do that. Now what information do you have for me?"

"It's not good Rosie, but it may not be your granddaughter."

Rosie asked, "Oh my God, what?"

"The one child who was ill and checked out at the hospital in Elyria, Ohio, was brought into a hospital in Toledo. She passed away from the respiratory complications she had and the adult male who brought her in disappeared."

Still holding the phone, but speechless, she heard Tony say, "Rosie, are you ok?"

She didn't answer, until Tony asked again, "Rosie, please talk to me, Rosie."

"Tony, I was told a few minutes ago about one of the children being very sick, but it was the little girl with red hair."

"Who told you that?'

"Tony, we'll stop at the office in Youngstown and I'll call you from there. I'll tell you all that I found out, but then we're driving straight through to Toledo. I have information that they stayed at a Howard Johnson's here in Grove City but I'm going to pass that up and head for Youngstown right away."

"At this point Rosie we can't be sure which child was ill."

"I know Tony, but it's not acceptable, whichever child it is."

"There's something else. We don't know if it's connected, but an eight year old girl has disappeared from the Toledo area, approximately three weeks ago."

"Three weeks ago, what makes you think they may be the same kidnappers?"

"From the only eye witness account, an old green car was seen in the area."

"That would mean they stayed around Toledo for some time."

"Rosie, the deceased child is being kept at the City Morgue under a Jane Doe, Case #147642."

"Tony, I'll call you when we get to Youngstown."

"Ok, and please keep your damn phone charged and on you at all times."

"I will, I promise, thank you Tony."

"Talk to you soon. Bye Rosie."

17

The drive to Youngstown took less than an hour and locating the FBI office was no problem at all. Rosie insisted that Juanita stay with the motor home and keep Sandy from getting into too much trouble, and protect all their belongings.

Getting through one security area to another even though Rosie had the agent's name was taking much too long for the ex-police officer. She decided to push a few buttons and raise a ruckus to see if that would speed things up a little.

Walking up to the receptionist who had told her to have a seat three times already, Rosie said, "Ok that's it, I've had enough of this shit. I've been sitting here forty-five minutes waiting to see Agent Richards, with important information about the kidnapping in Toledo. Now I've decided I'm leaving and you bunch of fools can figure it out on your own."

While waiting at the elevator, Rosie was approached by a man who identified himself as Agent Carroll and asked her if she would please follow him to a room down the hall. Rosie put her hands on her hips, shook her head, and then wiggled a finger at the man and said, "Look, unless you're taking me to see Agent Richards, you can go to hell, I have to get to Toledo."

The agent spoke softly and said, "Please Miss Castro, Agent Richards will join us in just a few minutes I promise. He has been in a meeting with the Bureau Chief and on a conference call with the Director."

Rosie stared at the man a few seconds and then told him, "I'll go with you, but if there is any more stalling bullshit, I'm out of here."

Sitting in the conference room for only a few minutes, Rosie was joined by a tall, blond haired, blue-eyed man who identified himself as Agent Ted Richards. Rosie stood and got right in the man's face and said, "You know Agent Richards, I have been waiting almost an hour to talk with you."

"I'm sorry Miss Castro. I've been on the phone with the Director, and with our friend Tony Servantes. We had a lot of information to exchange. Agent Servantes told me you have a picture of one of the kidnappers."

"Look Ted. May I call you Ted? I need to get on the road to Toledo."

"Please, not yet Miss Castro."

"Please, call me Rosie, Ted. What do you mean not yet?"

"We need to compare notes."

"I told you I have to get to Toledo to find out if the child in the morgue is my granddaughter."

"It's not Lisa in the morgue. The child's name is Elizabeth Schorr and she died from complications of pneumonia and her parents have been notified."

Breaking down in tears, Rosie uttered the words, "Thank God. Oh I'm sorry, I didn't mean it that way, and I feel so bad for her parents."

"I understand what you mean but I have to urge you to end your hunt for these sick individuals and go back home. Leave finding them to the professionals."

"So you already have a picture of them Ted?"

"No."

"Well I do."

The Agent said, "But Rosie."

"How about the license plate number and complete description of the car?"

"No, not quite," the agent said.

"What about the woman's artificial leg. I suppose you know about that also Ted?"

"No."

'His love of Mounds candy bars?"

"No."

Rosie laughed, "So much for the professionals, Ted."

"Rosie you don't understand, these people are dangerous."

"There's something you don't seem to understand Ted. That's my granddaughter with those sick bastards, and I am getting closer to them. So help me, I'm not quitting until I find them and get my granddaughter back."

"We believe they're heading for Chicago Rosie."

"And I believe they're heading for Nevada Ted."

"What makes you think its Nevada?"

"One of the maps they bought in Pennsylvania was a Nevada map, and a bumper sticker on their rear bumper said, "Lucky Me, I spent one whole night in Pahrump Nevada."

"That sticker could have been on there from a previous owner."

"I don't think so, not in the way he has taken care of that car and kept it in squeaky clean condition, from what I've been told."

"End this Rosie, and let us take care of the investigation, please."

"Ted, here is my cell number, if you want to share any new information with me, please call."

"I can't change your mind huh?"

As she stood up and offered her hand to shake, she said, "No you can't Ted. Remember, I am a trained professional too and I won't quit. Now, do you want a copy of that bastard's ID and license plate or not?"

The agent took the copies from Rosie and told her, "Agent Servantes asked if you would please call him before leaving the office."

While she waited for the agent to finish making copies, she tried calling Tony, but it went to voicemail.

It took only a few minutes for the agent to copy the information, and then she left the office. As she exited the building, she saw Juanita sitting on a bench with Sandy on her leash in the little park area adjacent to the Government building.

Sitting down on the bench next to her daughter, Rosie put her arm around her and said, "Lisa is still safe and we are getting closer, but we need to get on our way if we're going to catch them."

Rosie held her daughter's hand and told her about the other little girl and what had happened to her and that Lisa was still alive. Juanita cried and

Rosie held her close and said, "We will find Lisa and she will be fine, trust me."

Finding a gas station and filling up the van, checking things like water and oil, Rosie followed the signs to the Interstate. Before pulling onto the highway Rosie pulled over and told Juanita, "Sweetheart, how about you drive for a while. I'm going to look at the map and make a sandwich. Can I get you something dear?"

"No thanks mom, but the driving will help take my mind off of things a little."

18

Leaving Youngstown still heading west on I-80, Juanita was driving as Rosie plotted their course on the map. They had been on the road only about three hours when they entered an area very dense with large trees and no sign of buildings or people. An old Ford van sat parked on the side of the road with a young woman standing next to it. She was waving her arms franticly for the motor home to stop and assist her.

Rosie, by this time had lain down on the bed and was taking a short catnap, but when the motor home slowed and pulled off the road, she woke asking her daughter, "Why are we stopping?"

Juanita said, "There's someone in trouble Mom, and she looks like she could use a ride."

Before Juanita could get up from behind the wheel, the side door of the motor home was pulled open with a loud crunch. Standing in the doorway was a big dirty looking man holding a shotgun who said, "Going my way?"

The young woman, who had been standing next to the Ford van, was just a decoy to get someone to stop and render assistance.

As the big burley looking man stepped into the motor home, his weight, that must have been 275 pounds, shook the vehicle and started Sandy barking uncontrollably.

Rosie had just come out of the rear bedroom and asked, "Just what do you want?"

He said, "Just a ride little lady, all your money, and all your valuables." Then he started laughing. "Just sit your ass down and shut the fuck up."

Rosie by this time had grabbed Sandy by her collar, but the man said, "Shut that mutt up, or I will."

The young woman had come into the motor home smiling, "This is very nice. I'm going to enjoy riding in here."

Juanita started screaming as the man pointed the shotgun at her. He told her, "Shut up lady, or I'm going to get blood all over that dash board when I blow your head off."

Rosie said in a very calm voice, "Look, there's no need for violence, we'll give you anything you want."

The big jerk said, "Now that's a smart woman there. So get to it and get me all your valuables and cash and put them on the table."

Rosie walked back into the bedroom and brought out a small jewelry case and placed it on the table.

Sitting down at the table the man placed his shotgun next to the case, trying to open it, and asked, "Where's the key lady? It's locked"

Rosie said as she turned to the kitchen cabinet, "Oh I'm sorry, let me get you the key."

Sitting back stretching and clasping both his hands behind his neck, he looked at his girlfriend and said; "I told you this was going to be easy?"

As Rosie's hand came out of the cabinet drawer, she was holding her 38 Smith and Wesson and pointed it at the man's head saying, "Don't do any thing stupid, or you're going to die right where you sit."

Suddenly his girl friend screamed, but Rosie never took her eyes off the big man.

Rosie told Juanita, "Slowly reach for the shotgun sweetheart." Then she told the young woman, "Sit down next to your boy friend and shut the hell up."

The idiot did not believe that Rosie would actually shoot him, so he started to rise up slowly from the seat.

Rosie said, "Don't be a fool, sit down."

Not believing her he said, "Girly I don't think you have the guts to shoot, so why don't you just hand me that gun before you get hurt."

Rosie smiled and said, "Asshole, if you don't sit back down, I'll show you what kind of guts I have, before you die."

The man, still not believing Rosie, continued to get up from the table, and with no hesitation Rosie squeezed the trigger and put a bullet in the man's right shoulder.

As he flopped back in the seat he said, "Are you crazy lady, you shot me?"

"Try getting up again shithead and I'll put one right between your eyes."

With the sound of the gunshot, Sandy had started barking again and Juanita tried to calm her down. Rosie told her daughter, "Sweetheart, get the cell phone and call 911 and give them our location and tell them what happened."

"But Mom, I don't know our location."

Looking at the bleeding big man, Rosie asked, "Ok jerk, how do we let the paramedics know where you're at, or do I just shoot your ass again and throw you out the door?"

"Just tell them we're about two miles east of the 80 and the 480 junction, near Ridgeville."

After a brief explanation to the 911 operator, Juanita said, "They're on the way mom."

Juanita had handed the intruder a wet towel to hold against his wound to slow down the flow of blood and then went outside to wait for the ambulance. Ten minutes later, the paramedics arrived at the scene followed by two police cars. After a brief explanation by Juanita, the first officer slowly entered the motor home with his weapon in hand and saw Rosie pointing her gun at the man behind the table.

Very calmly the officer said, "I have it from here ma'am, please lower your weapon and tell me what's going on here."

As Rosie lowed her weapon the wounded man said, "She's crazy officer, the dumb bitch shot me for no reason."

Rosie pointed to the shotgun sitting beside her and said, "First thing you should know officer is that I'm a retired detective from New Jersey. The fool with the hole in his shoulder along with the other fool sitting next to him tried to rob us and threatened to shoot my daughter. I got hold of my gun and fired in self defense as he attempted to come at me after I had warned him twice."

The officer asked, "Can I see some ID please Ma'am?"

After showing the officer her retired police officer ID along with her gun permit and driver's license, the officer called in his back-up deputy to place the wounded man in handcuffs. Once the man was under control, the deputy took him out to the paramedics to tend to his wound.

As the paramedics and one of the police cars that had arrived on the scene pulled away, the remaining police officer sat down with Rosie to hear an explanation of the facts. After going through the details once, the officer had her explain all over again with more detail of what had transpired. Rosie was told by the officer that she would have to remain in town until a judge could determine if the shooting was warranted.

Rosie said, "Warranted, you want to know if saving our lives by shooting that piece of shit was warranted?"

"I didn't mean it that way ma'am, but being an ex-police officer yourself, you must understand that I'm just following proper procedure set up by the department."

Looking at the officer's nametag on his uniform, Rosie said, "Officer Martin, as I told you before, we are tracking kidnappers of my granddaughter, and the longer we stay around here the farther they get away."

"Miss Castro, you must come down to the station house and explain it to my chief. Let him make the decision as to whether you can go, he's a fair man with a lot of common sense."

"Ok officer, we'll follow you in."

"It's only a couple of miles up the road and maybe we can resolve all this quickly."

"Officer Martin, thank you for the quick response."

"Miss Castro, because there was a shooting I can't promise anything, but I'll see what I can do to get you back on the road."

Rosie smiled and said, "Thank you."

19

The ride into the city of Elyria was not uneventful in itself. Before arriving at the Elyria Police Station, Rosie watched as the police car they were following suddenly turned on its flashing red lights and siren, then sped up and made a very abrupt right turn on to Main Street.

Not knowing for sure if she should follow the speeding police car or go on her own and try to locate the police station, Rosie chose to follow the black and white with the flashing lights. A half-mile down the road the police car pulled over in front of the Main Street Food Mart, joining two other police cars with their lights flashing.

The officers from the other two vehicles were standing with their service revolvers drawn and aimed at the driver of a black SUV, parked near the front wall of the parking lot.

Officer Martin removed his service revolver from its holster and slowly walked toward the front of the vehicle saying, "Put your hands on the steering wheel and don't make any quick moves."

The man behind the wheel obeyed the commands of the officer and placed both hands on the steering wheel as directed. As one of the other officers walked to the driver's side of the car, a shot from across the parking lot struck him in his left leg dropping him to the ground.

Officer Martin taking careful aim fired two shots striking the man who fired the shot, with both bullets entering the man's chest center mass. Next, pointing his revolver at the man in the SUV, the officer said, "Do not move a muscle or a finger, or you will be joining your friend on a trip to the morgue."

Watching both shootings from their position parked behind the police car, Rosie and Juanita noticed a third suspect holding a gun in his hand, running from the front door of the Food Mart.

Trying to get Officer Martin's attention by first blowing her horn, Rosie then backed up her vehicle and drove around the side of the building and watched as the man got into a Chevy van and drove off. With Juanita's marker pen in her hand, Rosie wrote down the license plate number on her hand and then returned to the front of the building to join the officers.

As Rosie and Juanita exited the motor home, Officer Martin said in a loud commanding voice, "Get back in your vehicle ma'am".

Trying to explain what they had witnessed, each time she tried to speak, the officer said, "Just get back in your vehicle ma'am, this is a crime scene."

Putting her hands on her hips, Rosie yelled, "Get your head out of your ass Martin, a third suspect just took off down the road in a white van."

Finally paying attention to what Rosie had to say, he asked, "Which way did he go? What did he look like?"

"He was a white male around thirty, about six foot, 175 pounds, dark brown hair, blue jeans, and a light gray sweat shirt."

After calling in the report of the shooting and giving the description of the third suspect, Officer Martin said, "Thank you Ma'am. That was a good description."

Rosie said, "That's police training for ya."

Officer Martin asked, "What else did you notice Ma'am?"

Rosie thought a few seconds and said, "The Chevy van was a dirty white piece of crap with a logo on the rear doors. I think it said Rumson's Cleaners and it was about twenty years old."

"You didn't happen to get the license plate number, did you?"

Looking at the palm of her left hand, she said, "How's this work? HAW347. They were Illinois plates."

Officer Martin got back on the radio and relayed the plate number and description of the van. The paramedics arrived at the scene and started immediately to help the wounded officer. As for the robbery suspect who was shot by the officer, it was a job for the coroner. The suspect, who had been in the SUV, was now in custody, handcuffed and seated in the back seat of the police car.

With the description Rosie provided Officer Martin, an all points bulletin went out to apprehend "with extreme caution, armed and dangerous."

The manager of the Food Mart had come out of the store to talk with the officers. He let them know that no one in the store had been hurt and asked if the stolen money had been recovered.

Rosie and Juanita sat in the motor home until Officer Martin finished taking notes from witnesses in the food store. Then they were instructed to follow him once again to the police station.

Following closely behind the police car, the motor home soon pulled into the police parking lot next to the city hall building. Rather than leaving Sandy in the motor home, Juanita put a leash on her and said, "Come on girl, we're going to meet some nice people."

The police chief, Wilbur R. Denton, had just returned from a meeting with the Mayor and met Officer Martin, Rosie, and Juanita as they entered the Police Station. The chief had full knowledge of the robbery and shootings at the Food Mart, but wanted to hear the officer's version of the incident before meeting with the DA.

Rosie and Juanita had been taken to an interrogation room where their statements on the shooting in Rosie's motor home were being recorded. When a new line of questioning started about the Food Mart shootings, Rosie said, "I think before we give our account of what happened at your shootout scene, Officer Martin, my daughter and I need to have a little talk in private, so we'll wait on our statement for now."

Officer Martin asked her, "Ma'am what do you mean by that, are you refusing to give an official statement of what you both witnessed?"

Rosie smiled and said, "I think I'll wait to see just how good my memory is on who shot first at the market."

It took only a few seconds before the door opened and a Lieutenant stepped in and said, "Officer Martin, I've been informed by the DA to tell you to stop your questioning of Miss Castro for now."

Rosie was asked if she would like something to drink, and told that the chief would be with her in just a few minutes.

20

Rosie's statement of, "We'll wait on that for now," caused all kinds of commotion in the department. It had quickly brought the DA to the Police Station and then the Interrogation Room, in only about fifteen minutes along with the Chief.

After the DA introduced himself, the Chief informed Rosie that the man she shot, along with his female accomplice were wanted for robbery and assault on several victims, one of which was still in the hospital in a coma.

First thanking her for her assistance in the apprehension of the couple, the chief then told her the DA had some questions for her.

The DA, Richard Steele, asked, "Miss Castro, why are you refusing to give your account of the police-involved shooting at the Food Mart?"

"Mr. Steel, I'm not refusing to answer any questions or to give a statement of what we witnessed."

"But when Officer Martin asked you for an official statement, you refused. You did refuse, we have that on tape. What is your reason for not giving a statement on the Food Mart shooting?"

"That's not quite correct sir. What I need from you is a little co-operation and professional courtesy concerning my shooting of that big dumb ass that tried to rob me, and also threatened to shoot my daughter."

"What exactly do you need Miss Castro?"

"We have been tracking the kidnappers of my granddaughter for a while now, following leads of witnesses who have come in contact with them. We are getting closer to them all the time as long as we keep moving. If we have to stay around here until that big jerk and his girl friend goes on trial, we could lose the kidnappers' trail."

"Miss Castro, I think we can work something out, but I need to have a talk with the judge who will be assigned to their trial."

"And how long will that take Mr. Steele?"

"I'll call him as soon as I leave this room, but I won't lie to you, it could take a couple days to work things out Miss Castro."

"We don't have a couple of days Mr. Steele."

"Sorry, that's the best I can offer you for now. You must understand how serious your situation is. After all Miss Castro, you did shoot someone and we must check your story and your ID out thoroughly."

Looking at the DA, the Chief, and then Officer Martin, Rosie said, "I do understand, so where can we park our motor home for the next couple of days while you check us out?"

"Miss Castro, if it's okay with the Chief, you can park at the rear of the parking lot that you're parked in now."

The Chief spoke up and said, "That will be fine Miss Castro. Now can we get on with your statement about the Food Mart shooting, and just what you witnessed?"

"I wouldn't have it any other way Chief."

"Fine, for a minute there I thought we might have to charge you with being an uncooperative witness."

Rosie said, "Please Chief, I never said I wouldn't cooperate, I just needed you to cooperate to help all involved."

As the DA smiled, he asked, "Tell me again Miss Castro, why was it they forced you into retirement, I think you missed your calling for moving further up the ladder."

Smiling, Rosie said, "Thank you Mr. Steele, I had my sight set much higher, but unfortunately fate had something else in store for me."

Before Rosie had a chance to stand, her cell phone started playing the song from the movie MASH, "Suicide is Painless", and she excused herself as she answered.

Seeing that the caller was Tony, she answered, "Hi Tony, I have so much to tell you but I'll have to call you back."

"Rosie no, I have so much to tell you also about the kidnappers."

Looking at the DA Rosie said, "I'm sorry Mr. Steele but I have to take this call now."

The DA waved his hand as to say, "Go on, it's okay."

Before he could ask where they were, Rosie told him she and Juanita were in a police station and couldn't talk for long.

Tony said, "What, Where?"

"It's okay Tony, I'll explain later. Now what is it that you need to tell me?"

"Rosie, we got another call from the kidnappers, but he refused to talk to anyone else but you."

"What did you tell him?"

"I told him you were checked in at the flight deck at Bellevue, for observation and alcohol withdrawal."

"You told him I was in the nuthouse ward at Bellevue Hospital, and he believed it?"

That brought a strange look from the DA and Chief, but they said nothing.

Tony continued, "Hey, you've been drinking like a lush for the past few years. What's so hard to believe?"

"Oh screw you Tony. What was his response?"

"He laughed and said that was where you belonged, and then hung up."

"When I catch up to him I'm going to make him eat those words. What about Lisa?"

"He refused to talk and just hung up."

Rosie said, "That asshole."

"Yeah, yeah, now tell me where you are and what you have been doing."

"Well right now I'm at the Elyria Police Station in Ohio."

"What the hell are you doing there?"

"Two reasons. One is that we witnessed a super market hold-up and a police shooting of a suspect in the robbery. Second, I shot some dumb ass who was trying to rob us on the highway when we stopped to help him and his girl friend."

"Wait a minute, you shot someone?"

"Yeah Tony, I shot someone. The bastard was holding a shot gun on us, and when he put it down, I shot him when he came after me."

"Are you alright?"

'We're fine Tony. Juanita and I have to remain here for a couple of days until a judge gives us the okay to get back on the road."

"Where the hell is Elyria again?"

"It's a nice little town about twenty-five or thirty miles west of Cleveland."

"You keep your ass there, and I'll be there tomorrow."

"Tony that isn't necessary, we're fine I told you."

"Never mind Rosie, I'll be there tomorrow. I have a shitload of leave time coming to me and I could use a vacation. Keep your cell phone turned on."

"But Tony."

"No buts, I'll be there tomorrow, goodbye."

Getting off the phone, Rosie looked at the DA as he asked, "Boyfriend?"

Rosie said, "Friend with the FBI."

The DA said, "I didn't mean to eavesdrop, but it sounded a little more personal than FBI business."

"It's okay Mr. Steele he's an old friend who worries a lot. He said he'll be here tomorrow."

The DA said, "I'd like to talk with him when he gets here."

"I'm sure he'll want to talk with you also Mr. Steele. Now, can you recommend a place to get a nice home cooked meal and would you give me directions to the hospital and to the Howard Johnson's Motor Lodge?"

The DA asked, "Hospital?"

"Yes, I need to check out some information about the kidnappers stopping there for one of the kidnapped children who was sick when they came through town a few weeks ago. They spent four days around the area staying at the HJ."

The diner that was recommended to them served real home made style meals and they made the best of it. Sandy also benefitted by getting a nice sized soup bone to keep her busy for awhile.

After the meal Rosie drove to the local hospital to see if she could get some information about the man and woman who brought the young girl to the emergency room for treatment.

Since it was after 8PM there were only a few people on duty and no one remembered the old couple or the sick child. Rosie decided to wait until the next day and return when there were more people on duty.

Rosie and Juanita returned to the motor home to get some much needed rest.

21

The next morning with the sun shining brightly, Rosie had just come back from her walk to a diner a short distance from the Police Station. Juanita sat on the bed writing a letter to her friend back in New York. Rosie sat at the table sipping her coffee and reading the morning paper, when a knock came at the door. Looking out the window before unlocking and opening the door, she said, "Tony, how the hell did you get here so fast?"

"That's it, no nice to see you or I missed you so much."

Rosie said, "Yeah, yeah, I missed you so much. Now tell me, how did you get here so quick?"

"I know people sweetheart, people with airplane connections, so I made a couple of calls. And guess what, Bingo, I flew into Cleveland early and then rented a car."

As Rosie hugged her old friend, she asked, "You're not going to start that crap about me going back home are you?"

"Don't take this the wrong way, but you're like an old hound dog that got the scent of something you've been after a long time, and it would kill you to quit now."

"Old hound dog? I'll show you how an old hound dog can bite you on your ass."

"Should I consider that foreplay?"

As a big smile appeared on her face, Rosie said, "You wish."

"So tell me, who was this poor soul you shot?"

Standing in the doorway to the bedroom, Juanita answered that question.

"Tony, he was a big scary guy who was going to hurt us, and I was so afraid."

As Tony walked over to her, Juanita started to cry and he hugged her, "It's okay you're safe now, he won't hurt you anymore."

Those tears that Rosie saw from her daughter really hurt her and she paid attention to Tony's reaction. "Juanita, why didn't you tell me how you felt?"

"I couldn't Mom. I was trying to be strong for you and give you support, but I was so scared."

Rosie walked over to her, took a small towel off the counter top and wiped the tears away and said, "Honey, I want you to know that I was scared too. This is only the start, and there most likely will be more trouble ahead."

Before Rosie could say another word, Juanita said, "Don't you dare Mom, I know what you're thinking. Don't you dare tell me to go home, I need to be with you, and you need me to be with you, so I'm staying until we get my baby back."

Rosie's cell phone started playing her favorite tune and she answered it as Tony asked, "Suicide is Painless?"

"Hi, this is Rosie."

"Good morning Miss Castro, it's Richard Steele. Can you come to my office so we can talk?"

"Sure, what's up sir?"

"Chester Boranski, the man who tried to rob and kidnap you on the highway, just agreed to a plea bargain, which will keep him behind bars for a few years, depending on the mood of the judge."

"A few years that's it? That bastard should do at least twenty. How could you make a deal that would let him off so lightly?"

"Miss Castro, it's a plea bargain. If we went to trial, and you for some reason did not appear as a witness for the prosecution, he could walk on those charges."

"Mr. Steele, I'm sorry. What else do you need me to do?"

"Just need one more statement from you and your daughter, and then you can be on your way."

Rosie asked, "How about an hour from now, my friend from the FBI just arrived?"

"That will be fine, please bring him with you. Shall we say 11:30?"

"Okay, 11:30 it is. See you then."

As she hit the END button on her cell, Rosie looked up to see both Juanita and Tony staring at her.

Rosie said, "Juanita. That was the DA, Richard Steele. He would like to see us in his office in an hour to give him one last statement before we leave town. Tony, he would like to talk with you also."

"We can leave?" Juanita said.

"Yes. The asshole who tried to rob us took a plea bargain deal, and he's going to jail for a few years. Once we give a final statement, and visit the hospital again, we're heading for Toledo this afternoon."

Tony asked, "Toledo, why are you going to Toledo?"

"That's where the hospital is where Elizabeth Schorr died. We need to go there and try to get information on the kidnappers. You're not going to start questioning how I conduct my investigation are you? Because if you are, you can get back in your car and go back to that airport? "

"Rosie, I came here to give you some moral support not to give you any shit, so put your claws away."

"I'm sorry Tony, I'm just tired and lashing out. How about joining Juanita and me in the DA's office while we give our statements and then maybe have lunch before we pay a quick visit to the local hospital here? After that we take off, is that okay with you?"

"How would you feel about me joining you and Juanita as a guest passenger in your wonderful home on wheels for a few days?"

"I don't know if that's a good idea, besides, what about your job?"

"I have about six weeks of vacation time accrued and if I don't start using some of it soon, I may lose it."

"I don't know Tony?"

Juanita spoke up, "Mom, don't I get a vote here?"

"Sure you do sweetheart. What do you think about Tony coming with us for a while?"

"Mom, I think it's a great idea. Having Tony with us will make it easier to get information and you know we'll be safer."

"Well that's it, looks like it's three to nothing in favor of you coming along darling. Juanita and I can share the bedroom, and you get to sleep on the couch."

"Maybe I can help with some of the driving?'

"What about your car Tony?" Juanita asked.

"I'll find the local rental agency and turn it in. Now how about some coffee before we go see that DA?"

22

The meeting in the DA's office got off to a good start with introductions all around. Everyone was informed that the official statements were being recorded and no one had a problem with it. It took a little over two hours, with Rosie and Juanita giving one more complete account of what happened in the motor home shooting.

The Food Mart shooting statement mostly came from Rosie, since she witnessed more than Juanita did. Tony, being there as a character witness for the two women, helped to corroborate Rosie's identity and her impeccable police record.

The first part of the meeting dealt with the attempted robbery and shooting in Rosie's motor home. The second group of questions was more extensive concerning the Food Mart police shooting.

With a signed agreement that Rosie and Juanita would return for the trial as a witness for the prosecution at a future date, the DA permitted the two women to leave the state.

Once they were told to be on their way and started walking, Rosie turned to Tony, "I've given it more thought Tony. I don't believe it's a good idea for you to come with us."

Juanita said, "Mom. I thought it was decided, Tony comes with us."

Tony spoke up "Rosie, don't be foolish. I can open doors for you that otherwise might stay closed."

"I just don't want any shit from you when it comes to making decisions Tony, I call the shots, me alone."

"Rosie, I promise you, I'll help if I can, but you call the shots. Just promise me one thing."

"What's that?"

"You won't let foolish pride or your ego keep you from asking me for help if you need it."

Rosie stared at him for a few seconds. "What are you friggin' crazy all of a sudden Tony? If I need some help or advice I'll ask. If not, I'll tell you to just sit there and keep quiet. Do we understand each other?"

"Sounds good to me, sweetheart."

Breaking out with a smile on her face, Rosie kissed him on the cheek and said, "Come on, let's go talk to some people at the hospital and maybe we can get to Toledo before it gets dark."

"Mom, we need to pick up a few more groceries before we take off for Toledo."

"Okay dear, how about you going back to the motor home and keep Sandy, company while Tony and I go do some shopping. Maybe it would be a good idea to take her for a little walk in the park before we leave."

As they walked, Tony told Rosie he had new information for her about the kidnappers. He said, "I got it just before I left New York but it hasn't been confirmed yet."

Rosie stopped walking and said, "When were you going to tell me? You've been here for hours and you just decided to let me know."

"So when did we have a moment alone to talk? I just got here and the call came for you to go to the DA's office. Besides, I wanted to call in again to confirm it before I let you know what I had."

"Okay Tony. What did you find out?"

Pulling out a note book from his pocket, Tony said, "The security camera at the hospital here in town showed the old Buick with New York license plates on it. The Toledo Hospital camera showed the vehicle with Ohio plates. We do know it's the same vehicle by other identifiable markings."

Rosie said, "Yes, I got a security picture at the hospital last night. That just proves that these people were prepared for their cross country trip well in advance."

"There's something else. The Bureau believes the car was spotted in Gary Indiana two weeks ago with Illinois license plates, but it might just be an attempt to collect the reward offered for information by someone who is aware of the description."

"Two weeks ago?"

"Yes, by a gas station attendant."

"Where the hell is Gary, Indiana?"

"It's just south of Chicago, between I-80 and Lake Michigan, about 400 miles from here."

"Well with that information, we're going to make a quick stop in Toledo, and then get our asses to Gary."

"Rosie, it may just be a false report."

Thinking about it for just a few seconds, Rosie said, "You got somewhere else to go? What the hell, it's a lead, and we have to follow up on it."

"But it could be a wild goose chase, how about I make a couple of calls and see if the report has any truth to it?"

"See that, we are a good team Tony."

23

While they did some food shopping, Tony made a call to the rental car agency, informing them that his rental car could be picked up at the Elyria branch of their company. His second call was to his bureau headquarters back in New York and was told to stay on the line. He had asked to speak with an agent friend of his. But to his surprise he was instead connected to his supervisor.

Tony was told that although his vacation time had been approved, involving himself in an ongoing investigation in his off time was not. He was also told that the Director of Operations would be calling him as soon as he returned from Washington, that he was not happy with his actions. Also there has been a new turn of events that needs to be dealt with involving Miss Castro.

"What's the new problem Gus?"

"The Director will be revealing that to you."

Tony's response was, "I want to thank you Gus for filling me in on the hometown news, but I'm on vacation, I'll talk to you soon." Then he ended the call.

When Tony got off the phone, Rosie asked, "So what was that all about?"

"I was told I should be expecting a call from one of my bosses, nothing to worry about."

With a couple of shopping bags filled with enough supplies to last them a few days, the couple walked at a speedy pace trying to get back to the motor home and get the show on the road.

While walking with Sandy at her side, Juanita started crying and sat down on a bench next to the motor home. She had just received a phone call from a bureau agent in New York who told her there was a problem. He told her, "The kidnappers, trying to get in touch with Detective Castro, called the FBI and instructed them that they wanted to talk with her immediately or they would break off all communications forever."

When Juanita saw Tony and told him about the call, he said, "That son-of-a-bitch, I was just on the phone with them and they didn't tell me."

As Tony started to punch in the number for his bureau supervisor, Rosie's cell phone went off.

An Agent Russel Taylor, who Rosie had never spoken to before, told her of the call from the kidnappers.

Telling him to hold on a second, she then asked Tony, "Do you know an Agent Russell Taylor?"

"Yes I do. Tell Russ that I'm here with you."

"Yes Agent Taylor, Tony Servantes is here and sends his regards."

"Miss Castro, may I speak with Agent Servantes please?"

"No, you can speak with me Agent Taylor, and don't give me any bullshit."

"Miss Castro, we've been contacted by the kidnappers and they made it very clear that they want to talk to you as soon as possible."

"Did you get a trace on where they were calling from?"

"Yes we did, but I can not give you that information."

"You better think real hard, Agent Taylor, about changing your mind on that. You either tell me now or this call is over."

"It was Davenport, Iowa, Miss Castro."

"Iowa?"

"Yes. The call was made from a pay phone outside of a convenience store, using a calling card purchased at the same location."

"They seem to just keep heading west."

"Yes, and we're trying to get ahead of them."

"Agent Taylor, how was the conversation ended? I mean what did the kidnapper say he was going to do?"

"He said he would be calling back in one hour, and if you were not available, you would never hear from him again."

"Agent Taylor, go ahead and give him my cell number and tell him I am visiting with relatives in New Jersey, feel him out and please try not to offend him."

"Offend him? Miss Castro, please put Agent Servantes on the phone, this is not a time for amateurs to get involved."

Rosie said, "Amateurs?"

"Yes ma'am. You are an amateur and this is a job for experienced investigators."

Again, but louder, Rosie said, "Amateurs? Listen you asshole. I have more experience in my shit-stools then you have in all of your brain."

Just then Tony grabbed the phone from Rosie's hand and said, "Russ, this is Tony, what the hell is going on?"

"Who the hell does she think she is talking to me like that?"

"It's okay Russ, she's a grandmother worried about her granddaughter. She is also a retired police detective with seventeen years of experience dealing with all types of criminals, now what's going on?"

"We received a call from the kidnappers, and he made it clear that if he didn't talk with Detective Castro, he would break off all future communications and she would never talk with or see her granddaughter again."

"So Russ, the last communication from them was from where?"

"We traced it to Davenport, Iowa."

"Has the Bureau sent in a team to check out the location?"

"They're on the way as we speak, but the suspects are probably on the move again."

"When they call again Russ, give the caller Miss Castro's cell number, and don't let on that she is any other place but New Jersey visiting relatives."

"Ok Tony, I'll call you on your cell as soon as we get the call from them."

Once Tony was off the phone, Rosie, kissed him on the cheek and said, "Thank you for sticking up for me."

After putting away the groceries, Rosie told Tony she would follow him to the rental car lot, and then hopefully they could get underway heading west.

"What about that quick stop at the hospital Rosie?"

"Yeah I guess we better get over there before it get's too late." Rosie then added, "Tony, you know I love you like a brother, but if you ever pull my phone out of my hand again, I'll smack you like you've never been smacked before. Do you understand sweetheart, because I promise you I will?" Then she smiled and hugged him.

24

After apologizing to Rosie for snatching the cell phone out of her hand, Tony drove to the rental company to turn in his vehicle. Although everything was handled very smoothly, another hour had gone by and it was almost 4PM. Tony tried to talk Rosie into staying one more night in town to get a fresh start in the morning but to no avail.

Rosie told him, "Tony, this bus leaves for the west with one quick stop at the hospital in just a few minutes. But if you like, I'm sure there is another bus heading back east if that's what you want."

"Rosie, you're the driver, I'm just along for the ride, so let's get the hell out of here."

After giving him a sarcastic little smile, she said, "All aboard."

"You mind if I sit next to you driver, so I can enjoy the scenery whatever I may be able to see in the dark?"

Rosie smirked and said, "Smart-ass."

After a quick stop at the local hospital that didn't reveal anymore to Rosie than she had gotten on her last visit, she said thank you and left.

Surprisingly the I-80 west had very light traffic and Rosie got up to the speed limit quickly. From the back of the motor home Juanita said, "Mom, I'm going to lie down for awhile."

"Okay, I'll wake you when we get to Toledo."

As they rode along, Rosie and Tony reminisced about years gone by, some good and some bad. It helped pass the time and before they knew it, two hours had gone by and they were in downtown Toledo. During the drive, Tony called Agent Taylor twice but there had been no further contact from the kidnappers. Rosie's phone never played her favorite song letting her know someone was calling either.

After getting directions at a gas station, Rosie drove to the Saint James Mercy Hospital. Because of the late hour, the person in charge of security had gone home for the day and the night man, Robert Doyle, could not answer the questions asked by Rosie or Tony. On the second attempt at trying to contact the chief of security, the night man was told that his boss would be there in approximately one hour.

Tony suggested that it might be a good time to return to the motor home and have something to eat since they hadn't eaten all day. Reluctantly Rosie agreed and told the night security man where they had parked their vehicle.

The security guard smiled and pointed at the monitors suspended from the ceiling above the desk and said, "Ma'am, I can see your vehicle clearly from here. I watched as you drove in the lot and parked. By the way, you can't park there Ma'am, you need to move to the rear lot."

Rosie said, "Listen Mister Rent-a-cop, I'm only going to be there until your boss gets here and gives me a little information, then we're gone."

The guard got irritated and said, "Lady, I don't give a damn if you're only going to be there five minutes, I'm just doing my job. Now move it or I'll have it towed."

Not used to being talked to like that, Rosie started to open her mouth as Tony cut her off and said, "Bob, we will move the vehicle as soon as we can. Thank you for your help. Please let your boss know that we will be waiting for him in the back parking lot. Here's my cell number."

"And who are you sir?"

Holding up his ID, Tony said, "FBI, Bob, just ask him to call and we'll come back in."

While mumbling a little under her breath, Rosie stared at Tony, but didn't say anymore as they left the security office."

All during the walk back to the motor home Rosie never said a word to him. Standing in front of the door before going inside, she turned and faced Tony, "Thank you." Then she opened the door and went in before he could say anything in response.

Juanita was sitting at the table eating a sandwich and when she saw her mom and Tony come in. She said, "Mom, I thought you were going to wake me when we got here. You didn't leave me a note or anything. I was so worried."

Before Rosie could answer, her phone started playing Suicide is Painless, and as she said hello, Tony's phone also started buzzing.

The caller on Rosie's phone said, "Detective Castro, so nice to talk with you again."

"Who is this?" As if Rosie didn't know.

"This is your granddaughter's guardian, so shut up and just listen detective."

"Talk to me you bastard, where is my granddaughter?"

"She's safe and in good company, but are you?"

Rosie asked, "What do you mean am I?"

"Did you think I wouldn't find out Detective Castro?"

"Find out what?"

"I have spies all over Detective."

"For the last time shithead, I'm not a detective anymore. Those days are long over with."

"Are you having a nice trip, Detective Castro?"

"What do you mean?"

"How's the weather in Toledo right now?"

After a long silence and knowing that there was no sense in lying, Rosie answered, "A little cold, but getting warmer with each passing day."

Tony had told Agent Taylor that he would call him back as soon as Rosie was off the phone with the kidnapper, and asked him to try to pinpoint the location of the caller.

"Detective Castro, would you like to speak to your granddaughter?"

"Yes I would."

"I bet you would Detective, but now is not the right time. Maybe tomorrow we'll talk again."

With that the call was ended and Rosie let out a scream that immediately got Juanita's attention.

"What's wrong mom?"

"I want to kill that bastard. That's what's wrong."

After a short conversation with Rosie, Tony called Agent Taylor and informed him of the present situation. The agent told him that they couldn't get any additional information on the kidnapper's location, nothing more than they already knew. The two men agreed to stay in touch and inform each other if there were any changes in plans or circumstances.

Rosie sat twisting and crumbling a couple of paper towels that she had pulled off the roll on the counter. She kept saying over and over, "I will get that bastard and make him pay for what he is putting us through."

Juanita stood behind Rosie with her hands on her mom's shoulders trying to comfort her, as the tears rolled down her cheeks. She said, "They're bad people mom, but as long as Lisa is still safe we just need to keep going forward."

Getting up slowly from the table, Rosie told Juanita and Tony, "I think I'll lie down for a while, please wake me when the Security Chief gets here."

Tony took a loaf of bread off the counter, removed two pieces, looked at Juanita, and asked her, "How about another sandwich?'

Juanita smiled and said, "Tony, let me make the sandwiches. You sit and relax a few minutes; I need something to occupy my mind."

Tony thanked her and as he moved to sit on the couch, there was a knock on the door.

25

Opening the door, Tony asked the uniformed man who was standing there to come in, once he identified himself as Chris Bradley, chief of security at the hospital.

Rosie had only a chance to close her eyes for a few minutes when she heard the knock on the door. She was up and walking to the table before the chief cleared the doorway.

Making the introductions, she first introduced her daughter Juanita, Agent Tony Servantes of the FBI and herself. After a brief conversation, the chief suggested that they all go inside to the hospital security office and view some tapes and still shots. The Chief told them that all of the security footage had previously been shown to the FBI agents who visited weeks earlier.

Tony said, "Chief, I haven't eaten all day, you mind if I bring my sandwich with me?"

"Sure, as long as you eat it before you get in the front door or you'll have to go finish it in the cafeteria. It's hospital policy."

The walk to the hospital front doors took only a few minutes and before they entered, Tony had finished his sandwich and was wiping the mustard off his mustache with his handkerchief. Inside the front doors standing by the information counter, the night guard asked, "You want me to remain here Chief?"

"Yes Robert, just make your regular rounds. I'm sure I can handle things with these folks in the office."

As they followed the chief down the hall to a room that had, "Hospital Security" on a hanging sign, Chief Bradley said, "Next doorway folks, the one that says "PRIVATE" on it, I'll open it from inside this room and let you in."

Entering the room, it was obvious that it was used for viewing all the camera monitors that were set up all over the hospital grounds and the interior of the building.

The Chief said, "Have a seat folks while I set things up. It will only take a few minutes."

Watching the sweeping monitor that covered the front door, Tony noticed that when it pointed at the information counter, the night man Robert was nowhere around.

Rosie pointed to a monitor #6 at the end of the row that happened to be sweeping the hallway outside of the security office and the door marked "PRIVATE." She noticed the night guard listening with his ear pressed to the door.

Quietly, Tony waved to the Chief and pointed to the monitor. They watched as the Chief opened the door quickly and asked, "What the hell are you doing Robert?"

"Sorry Chief my curiosity just got the best of me, I am part of the security force here you know."

"I'll fill you in later. Now get back to your rounds."

Closing the door, the Chief said, "Sorry about that folks. He's a new man who has only been here a short time and from the looks of it, he won't be here much longer. Now let me show you what I got."

The tapes that the chief played showed the old Buick parking in the side lot. A tall elderly man was getting out of the vehicle and opening one of the rear doors. He then carried a small child through the doors of the Emergency Room. Also it showed a woman in her mid to late fifties, walking with a second child, who at times had to be tugged at to walk side by side with the woman.

Rosie, who had been sitting down watching the tape stood up and said, "So that's what that bitch looks like."

Tony noticed how the woman limped and pointed it out to Rosie, also that the child being tugged was Lisa. It was a good thing that Juanita had stayed behind in the trailer because the video that they were viewing would have disturbed her very much.

The mean spirited woman stood about five foot ten, with dark hair, weighed approximately one hundred and seventy five pounds and had a sour look on her face, as if she had just eaten a lemon. At one point during the walk to the hospital, the elderly woman smacked the child and yelled at her causing her to be partially dragged until she cooperated.

While sitting in the emergency waiting room, Lisa continued to cry and the woman became obviously annoyed. Again grabbed and jerked the little girl by her arm, and then they returned to the car. There was no telling whether she hit Lisa once back inside the old Buick.

Rosie was having a hard time controlling her temper as she called the couple many names in Spanish. Tony said, "Please Miss Castro, try to sit and continue watching."

In the Emergency Room the man was viewed at the check-in window as he talked with the receptionist with a full frontal shot.

The man was in his early to mid sixties, gray hair, about six foot two and he weighed about two hundred and twenty five pounds, with a non-descript face. He looked much older than the photo on the license that they had seen.

Rosie said, "Please stop and rewind if you would Chief. I'd like to take another close look at his features."

"I can do better than that Miss Castro."

Rewinding and stopping with a full frontal shot, the chief went over to the computer that was hooked into the system, cleaned up and enhanced the picture, then moved to the printer and pushed print. An 8x10 picture came out that was so clear you could see the unshaven stubble on his face.

Even Tony was surprised at the quality of the picture and said, "What kind of system is that? You should see some of the crap shots we have to work from sometimes and we're the FBI."

The Chief told him, "My brother-in-law is a computer wiz and this is all his doing. I'll give you his number before you leave."

Rosie looked carefully at the photo and said after a while, "I have no idea who this guy is or why he seems to know me so well?"

Watching six different tapes of six days, it appeared that the child that was brought into the hospital never left. At least not with the tall man who gave his name as Brian Reese if that was his real name. That was the name he used on the admitting forms for the child he brought in and declaring himself the grandfather and legal guardian. The Chief had all the forms and files that were attached to the child that was admitted.

Next the Chief said, "I have some photos of the child that may be disturbing to you that were taken in the morgue, after she succumbed from her illness."

Looking at a photo of the dead child on #1 monitor, Rosie thought she noticed something peculiar. She asked the chief if he could put a photo of the child at the time of admitting on #2 monitor at the same time. Next Rosie asked if the Chief could zoom in on the left calf just below the knee on both children, clear and enhance and then print them.

With both pictures side by side lying on the table, Rosie asked, "Do you all see what I see? That's not the same child, that large mole isn't there below the knee on the left leg."

Downloading and printing out additional enhanced pictures, it became even more obvious that the two minors in the photos were not the same person.

Tony asked the Chief to please install the last two tapes he had of the kidnapper's vehicle in the parking lot and zoom in on the occupants.

Rosie asked, "What is it you think you saw Tony?"

Tony said, "Just fishing sweetheart, just fishing."

After a few stops and rewinds, Tony asked the Chief to zoom in and enhance a picture for him. The picture showed two children looking out the rear window of the old Buick, one was Lisa and the other was unmistakably Elizabeth Schorr, alive and well.

Juanita, who had joined the group in the security office, gasped and said, "Oh my God, she's alive."

Somehow the kidnappers were able to manipulate the facts convincing everyone, including hospital staff that the child who was first brought into the hospital died and was now lying in the morgue. The reasoning was still not understood but it was very clear that Elizabeth Schorr's parents had to be contacted immediately.

The Chief was on the phone so quickly calling the head of hospital operations and he was heard saying, "I don't give a damn what you're doing, we have a serious situation here Peter. You better get your ass down here just as quick as you can."

After printing out a dozen different pictures, Rosie and Tony agreed that they needed to get back on the road and get a little closer to the kidnappers. Tony made a call to Agent Taylor and informed him of the new findings. The agent told him he would be picking up his partner and heading to the hospital.

"Sorry we won't get to meet with you," was expressed by Tony, "But we need to get to Gary Indiana."

"You need to remain at the hospital Agent Servantes, until we have a chance to go over all the new found evidence."

"Not a chance Russ, I'm on vacation. Talk with the Security Chief at the hospital, he's a sharp guy and he has all the facts. I'll stay in touch."

Tony then hit the END button on his phone and put it in his pocket.

Looking at Rosie, Tony said, "Let's go."

Juanita was carrying the picture of her darling Lisa looking out the back window of the kidnappers' car and cried as she walked back to the motor home. Rosie put her arm around her and told her she loved her, and that it wouldn't be long until Lisa was with them again. As they opened the door to the motor home, Sandy came running out barking and then peeing next to the front tire of the vehicle.

Rosie started the engine and let it warm up for a few minutes before she told Tony and Juanita to buckle up because it was time to leave. Making a wide circle in the parking lot before pulling out of the driveway, Rosie slowly got the vehicle up to speed and headed towards the interstate.

Juanita had decided to make a pot of coffee as they traveled down Main Street, and Tony, with a smile on his face said, "I need to visit the john ladies, and then maybe get a few hours sleep."

Rosie yelled out for all to hear. "Remember the motor home rule."

Juanita asked, "And what rule is that Mom?"

Before Rosie could answer, Tony said, "I know, I know, no pooping in the motor home."

With everyone breaking out in laughter, it sure broke the ice. Even for just a few minutes.

Rosie's attention was on the road ahead so there was no way she could have noticed the black Toyota that followed behind them and was watching every move they made.

26

Rosie estimated the drive to Gary, Indiana was around two hundred and fifty miles. Looking at a possible four-to-five hour drive and once again arriving in a strange town after dark was getting to be a pattern that no one liked. After talking about it with Juanita and Tony, Rosie decided to find a place along the way to pull in, have something to eat, spend the night and get a fresh start in the morning. It was a plan everyone liked. Even Sandy seemed to know what was coming.

From the interstate a tall sign could be seen that read, "TYLER'S TRUCK STOP-GAS-FOOD and LODGING," and in small letters, "campers welcome."

The next exit was about two miles ahead so they would have to double back to get to the large truck stop.

Pulling off I-80 down the off ramp, Rosie noticed a vehicle exiting right behind them, but it didn't seem to mean anything at the time. Making a right turn on Porter Road and then another right on Crenshaw Drive, it took only a few minutes before they were turning into the truck stop and parking in the lot at the rear of the diner.

The black Toyota drove past the front of the motor home and parked in a very dark corner of the lot. Turning off the lights and motor, the driver just remained in the vehicle. Rosie, Juanita and Tony ventured into the diner and were welcomed by an older waitress who told them to sit wherever they liked.

The diner had such a warm and comfortable feel to it that no one was in much of a hurry to return to the tight quarters of the motor home. Rosie pointed at a nice large booth and then she asked the waitress, "Excuse me hon, where's the ladies room?"

The old fashioned counter, booths and even the uniforms worn by the waitresses had a feel of the forties or fifties. It was like being tossed back in time and it was a wonderful feeling for everyone. The seats in the booths were done in a soft and comfortable fire-engine red vinyl, the tables were bright white Formica and the floor was black and white squares of linoleum tiles.

The music on the juke box was Jerry Lee Lewis, singing "Great Balls of Fire."

The food cooking in the kitchen was sending out smells of desire and gave everyone a desire to overeat.

Rosie came walking back from the restroom with a big smile on her face. As she sat down she said, "Splashing some cold water on my face, being able to use a real nice clean restroom, and knowing that we are getting closer to our goal has made me feel much better. Now what is everyone going to have?"

Juanita said, "The waitress told us their freshly made meatloaf dinner is the specialty of the house.

Tony closed the menu he was holding and said, "Sounds good to me."

After stuffing themselves with homemade meatloaf, lumpy mashed potatoes, fresh corn, gravy, warm corn bread with honey butter and mountain high apple pie, they were done.

Juanita said, "Sandy, I'm sure, is waiting patiently to get out and go pee."

After spending two hours in the diner, the happy well fed three-some returned to the motor home to turn in for the night with cups of tea to go and a doggie bag for Sandy.

With the contents of the doggie bag quickly devoured by Sandy and a short walk around the parking lot, Juanita returned to the motor home. Rosie was already lying on the bed and Tony had fixed up the couch into a comfortable bed and was getting ready to lie down. Juanita locked the door behind her, said "Night all," and joined her mom in the bedroom.

Unaware that their every move was being watched by a pair of sharp eyes in the black vehicle, they all turned in for the night.

As the sun came up it was time to get back on the road to Gary, Indiana but before they started their trip Tony said, "Give me a few minutes and I'll be back with some fresh coffee and pastry."

Rosie asked, "Tony, would you make mine a Taylor Ham and egg on a Kaiser roll please?"

Tony laughed, "I'd be surprised if they know what Taylor Ham is Rosie, but I'll try."

Walking to the diner, Tony noticed the vehicles parked by the back wall of the parking lot but he just assumed they had come in late last night and there was no need to give them any further attention.

Returning to the motor home with coffee and a big bag of pastries and Rosie's sandwich, he found the women ready to go. Tony told Rosie, "Sorry sweetheart, just plain ham and eggs, they have no idea what Taylor Ham is out here.

It was obvious that Sandy had other plans instead of leaving right away because of her scratching at the door. Juanita said, "Okay girl, I think we can give you a few minutes to relieve yourself. Let's go baby, it's potty time. We'll be right back everyone."

Walking around the perimeter of the parking lot, Sandy left her scent in about six locations plus a healthy deposit in front of one of the cars. As luck might have it, Sandy's deposit had been dropped in front of the black Toyota. As Juanita bent down to pick it up in a plastic bag, she noticed a man behind the steering wheel wearing sun glasses and a baseball cap smiling back at her.

In the shadows it was hard to make out the man's features but it didn't seem important at the time. Heading back to the motor home, Juanita tossed Sandy's little gift to the truck stop into the trash dumpster, never giving the man in the car a second thought.

Rosie had started the motor home to let the engine warm up, so all systems were go and they were off again.

In just a matter of minutes the motor home was traveling 65 miles per hour heading west on I-80, and following at a safe and almost out of sight distance, lurked the black Toyota.

With light traffic congestion most of the way, they arrived in Gary in just under four hours.

Tony had talked to an Agent Jankowski who had supplied him with the address of the gas station where the suspects had been spotted. The agent agreed to meet him there in an hour.

The gas station, a small two pump facility off the main highway in a rural setting looked like a place that hadn't been upgraded since the depression in the 1930's.

Pulling up to the gas pump they were welcomed by a young man dressed in dirty coveralls who asked, "Can I help you Ma'am?"

Rosie smiled at the man and said, "You sure can, how about filling her up with premium and checking the oil."

Exiting the motor home, Tony spotted an older gentleman sitting inside the shop watching a small black and white TV that had rabbit ears for an antenna.

Tony approached him, "Good morning sir, could I talk with you for a few minutes?"

"Sonny, I would welcome it. Todd there is a fine young man and a good worker, but he don't talk much."

Tony handed the man a picture of the old Buick, then a picture from the hospital security camera of the kidnapper and asked, "Do you by any chance remember seeing this car and driver come through here a couple of weeks ago?"

The old guy said, "I sure do. That old Buick was a beauty. It ran real nice when he left here after Todd's working on it but the driver was a fool."

"What do you mean, he was a fool?"

"He wanted regular gas in that car and I told him it needed premium, higher octane you know. You need it for those old high compression engines but he said no. The damn fool wouldn't listen."

"So you remember the car well?"

"Todd there did a tune up on it, just barely ran when it came in. I told him it was because he was running that crappy low octane gas but the fool didn't want to listen."

Rosie joined Tony and said, "Good morning sir."

The old man stood up, offered his hand and said, "Please call me Tom, Ma'am, Thomas Evans. I wouldn't know how to act if you called me sir, just ain't me."

"Nice to meet you Tom, I'm Rosie, Rosie Castro."

Tony looked at her and said, "Rosie, Tom says he remembers the old Buick coming through here a couple of weeks ago, even worked on it."

"Now that's not true, Todd worked on it. I just sat here and watched and talked with that fool."

Tony went on asking, "Do you remember any of the other passengers in the vehicle?"

"I didn't catch your name mister. Are you with the police or something?"

"I'm sorry Tom, my name is Tony Servantes, and I'm an agent with the FBI."

"Oh, just like that other guy that came by asking questions. Some Polish guy who said he was with the FBI too."

"That would be Agent Jankowski, who should be here any minute now."

"Yep, that was his name."

"So Tom, do you remember any of the passengers?"

"That's easy Tony, there were no passengers he was all alone. He told me he and his family were staying at the motel down the road. It's Martha Grimley's place, called the Bear Claw Motel and Diner."

Juanita had come out of the motor home with Sandy following right behind her and from the rear of the shop a deep bark came from an old German shepherd. The Sheppard had been resting but was now interested in what was going on and the scent of Sandy. The two dogs sniffed at each other for a while and then Sandy walked to the side of the building and sprinkled a little on the dried up weeds.

The young man, who had just finished filling up the gas tank and checking the oil and water, came over and said, "It's all filled up ma'am, and every thing's fine under the hood. Anything else I can do for you?"

The old guy said, "Todd, these folks are with the FBI, like the other Polish guy who was here last week. They're interested in that old Buick and that fool who was driving it."

Before Todd could answer, a gray Chevy Impala pulled in with government license plates on it. The man got out and walked over to Tony and asked, "Agent Servantes?"

Tony held out his hand and responded, "Agent Jankowski?"

The agent then looked at Rosie and asked, "You are Miss Castro I presume?"

"You got that right mister FBI man. What else you got for me?"

Holding out his hand, "Miss Castro, I'm Special Agent Jankowski. Can we find a private place so we can talk?"

Tony said, "How about that picnic table sitting under the tree on the side of the building?"

27

Agent Jankowski looked at Tony when they first sat down, "Agent Servantes. My orders are to inform you to call your office. From what I've been told, you are in a lot of hot water for not responding to calls from the Director. Now let's get to the other subject in front of us."

As the conversations at the picnic table went on, the black Toyota sat parked almost out of sight with the driver watching through a pair of binoculars. Although the driver could not tell if there was any sense of urgency, he felt it was time to make a phone call to the owner of the old Buick.

Agent Jankowski told Tony and Rosie that he was aware that the suspects had stayed at the motel down the road, but the information he had on them was not very complete. The only two people the motel manager had come in contact with were the old man and a woman. The woman he assumed was his wife and no children were seen at all.

Tony asked Tom, the gas station owner and Todd, the mechanic, if they had any idea where the driver of the Buick might be headed.

Todd told him, "I don't know if it means much, but I did notice an old oil change sticker on the door post from Nevada."

"That could mean a lot." Tony said. "Do you remember where in Nevada it was?"

"It was spelled funny. Something like, Pathump or Pahump."

Agent Jankowski said, "Pahrump, it's a town about forty miles from Las Vegas."

"Yeah, that's it, a 76 station in Pahrump."

Tony asked, "Isn't that a little desert town with a small population?"

Agent Jankowski was on his cell phone calling his superiors with the new information and when he finished he asked Tony, "What's your next move Agent Servantes?"

Tony put his arms up and said, "You're talking to the wrong person Jankowski, Miss Castro is calling the next shots. Besides, I'm officially on vacation."

Rosie put her hand on Tony's shoulder and said, "Tony, I think we need to pay a visit to the motel down the road."

"Best offer I had all day sweetheart."

Shooting Tony a look that would melt an iceberg, Rosie said, "Tony, get your mind out of the gutter."

As Tony's complexion turned a bright shade of red, he tried to rephrase his statement but started to get tongue tied and stuttered like a young scared teenager.

Rosie took his hand, winked at him and said, "I'm only kidding sweetheart, but romance is so far from my thoughts right now."

"I didn't mean to---,"

"It's okay Tony."

Agent Jankowski interrupted the conversation by saying, "I have some additional information. We have a positive ID on the driver of the old Buick. His name is Brian Doyle. His last known address was in Billings Montana."

Rosie said, "Montana, I thought he had ID from New York?"

"He also had a driver's license issued to him in New York, Florida, Montana and Nevada."

Tony asked, "Doyle? Wasn't that the last name of the security guard at the hospital?"

Rosie thought a second and answered, "Yes, his name was Robert Doyle, may just be a coincidence though."

Agent Jankowski said, "If he's security, it must be on record. These days a person can't get a job in security without being thoroughly checked out. Give me the name of the hospital and I'll check it out myself and get back to you."

After thanking Tom and Todd for their most valuable information, Rosie told Tony, "Com-on hon, let's go see what we can find out at that motel."

After exchanging cell numbers with Agent Jankowski, he was back in his car and burning rubber heading back to his office.

28

With an appointment missed intentionally at the Mercy Hospital in Chicago for a repair on her prosthetic leg, the now very angry Miss Paxton was furious with her companion Brian.

Brian's only excuse was that there are hunters on the trail very close behind them. It was information supplied by the driver of the black Toyota.

Continuing to travel west on I-80, the old Buick made a fueling stop in Joliet, Illinois on their way to Davenport, Iowa.

Only a short distance behind, a mere forty miles, Rosie, Juanita, Tony and Sandy were just leaving Gary, Indiana with no idea how close they were. The information provided by the motel manager was that the old man, woman and the two children were heading for Mercy Hospital in Chicago.

For the first time someone actually saw and gave a complete description of everyone in the old Buick, and it didn't include a young boy who was also assumed kidnapped by the old couple.

With the new information, Rosie headed for Mercy Hospital, not knowing that they were headed in the wrong direction.

Tony was busy on his phone relaying the new information to his superiors, which in turn, contacted Bureau Chiefs in the Chicago area. By the time Rosie reached the hospital, the old Buick was halfway to Davenport.

Tony and Rosie questioned several hospital section chiefs and came up with nothing. After returning to the motor home, Rosie knew she had to make a decision. With no indication which way to travel next, she just used her best judgment and continued west on I-80.

With the anticipation of catching up to the kidnappers, hoping she was only a short distance behind them, Rosie pushed the motor home past its limits. At many times during their trip Rosie had the pedal to the metal and it was a little too much for the aging motor home. Her bad practice in driving resulted in an unexpected breakdown in the town of La Salle, Illinois approximately halfway through the state.

An engine water pump failure was unexpected. The extreme overheating of the engine caused by continuing to drive after the temp gauge pegged out stopped them in their tracks.

Rosie, Juanita and Tony were forced to spend the night in a motel next to a repair shop and it unfortunately allowed the kidnappers to gain another day eluding them.

Davenport, Iowa is located just west of the Mississippi River separating Illinois and Iowa and rather then spending the night in that beautiful city, the kidnappers decided to push on and continue to Des Moines.

After checking into their motel in Des Moines, Brian Doyle made several calls on his cell phone.

The first call was to an old friend in Billings, Montana. Doyle instructed him to feed out some false information that Doyle and his lady friend would be returning to Montana. He explained that he might be questioned by the local police or the FBI.

The second call was to the person driving the black Toyota, who was following Rosie and hopefully staying out of sight.

The third call was a little more involved with Rosie answering instantly as "Suicide is Painless" chimed in on her cell phone.

"Hello my dear detective, having a nice trip? I know you think you are going to catch up with us but you can forget that because we're too smart for you."

Trying to restrain herself a little, Rosie responded with, "Are you ready to stop running and turn yourself in you asshole?"

"Why detective, do I sense a little bit of anger in your voice?"

"The little bit of anger in my voice will disappear as soon as I can put a bullet in your heart you bastard."

"Are you enjoying your stay in La Salle detective?"

"You can tell your spy, whoever he or she is, they will also burn in hell with you along with that bitch you have as a partner in this horrible crime."

"Now, now detective, no need for all this name calling."

"Is my granddaughter safe along with the other little girl Elizabeth?"

"Oh, you figured out that the little Miss Schorr didn't die in the hospital. How clever detective."

Rosie tried to stay calm and said, "You and your partner are sick bastards. Who was that child in the hospital?"

"That's of no more concern to you Detective Castro."

"Why do you continue to call me detective?"

"Miss Castro, you will always be a detective in my eyes."

"Why can't you understand that I am retired from the police force?

He laughed and said, "Once a cop always a cop."

"Just know this: I will use all my training to find you and your partner. I will either kill you both or turn you over to the FBI so they can put you away for life."

Laughing loudly, he answered, "Do you really think you have any chance of finding us?"

"So tell me, are you heading for Billings or some other place to hide?"

"Billings?" he responded.

"Yes, you know your hometown, asshole."

Once again laughing loudly, Brian Doyle just ended the call.

Rosie looked at Tony and said, "We have got to find out who is following us. Those bastards know every move we've made."

29

The next morning, the bad news came to Rosie from the mechanic working on her motor home. He said, "Sorry lady, but one of your heads on the engine is cracked."

With a bit of anger and sarcasm in her voice she responded, "And what does that mean mister mechanic, in English please?"

"It means ma'am, you will be spending a little more time here than you expected."

"And how much more time would that be until you fix the head?"

He said, "The head can not be fixed. It will be about three or four days at least ma'am. A lot depends on the availability of another head for your engine."

"You're sure my head can't be fixed?"

"Absolutely ma'am."

Rosie said quite loudly, "SHIT"

He looked at her and said, "Excuse me ma'am?"

"I'm sorry, just thinking out loud."

Tony, who was standing next to Rosie, got just the slightest smile on his face and that was all Rosie needed to go off the deep end. She started bitching and complaining about everything that had gone wrong to that point.

Tony put his arm around her and said, "Come on babe, let's go see what the accommodations are at the motel for the next few days."

Juanita had taken Sandy for a long walk and was just returning to the repair shop when she noticed that same dull black Toyota parked down the street from the motel. She remembered it and its driver from the restaurant parking lot a few days ago.

Trying not to attract attention to herself, Juanita crossed the road and walked down a side alley to the next street.

While Tony and Rosie were standing just outside of the motel office, Juanita and Sandy approached and Rosie knelt down and called to Sandy. The dog was only about twenty feet away when she started running towards Rosie.

As Rosie pet and cuddled the dog, Juanita told Tony about the man in the black Toyota who was watching them.

Tony said, "Just go along with me, I'm going to hug you and turn you around so I can get a better look at the car. Don't point or look yourself."

As Tony hugged and spun Juanita around, Rosie asked, "What the hell are you two doing?"

Without breaking from his jovial moves, Tony said, "Rosie, don't look down the street but we are being watched by some guy in an old Toyota. Juanita remembers him from back at that restaurant parking lot. He's been following us for a long time."

"Hon, is it a dirty looking black Toyota Celica?"

"Yeah, it is."

"I noticed him when we pulled out of the truck stop just outside of Toledo but didn't spot him again."

"You two go to the room and I'll walk around back and come up from behind him."

"Oh so now you're taking charge and calling the shots?"

"No sweetheart, I need you to walk slowly to the room but don't go in yet, just stand and talk to each other,. This will keep his attention on you two while I come up behind him."

As Rosie and Juanita proceeded to do their part, Tony took the path Juanita had taken and came up behind the Toyota. As he got closer, Tony identified the driver and walked up with his revolver drawn and said, "Hi Bob, enjoying the sights?"

Bob Doyle, was caught completely off guard by Tony, and after telling him to place both hands on his head, Tony opened the driver's door and assisted him out.

Turning him around and facing him towards the car, Tony put handcuffs on him, then turned him back facing him and asked, "What the hell do you think you're doing?"

Bob Doyle just smiled at him with no response.

As Tony continued to question Robert Doyle, Rosie and Juanita ran quickly to his side with many questions for the restrained man.

Tony said, "Rosie, wait."

Calling his supervisor back in New York, Tony was instructed to call the Peoria branch of the bureau and then call the local authorities and let them take over all questioning. While making his calls, Rosie decided to take things into her own hands and ask a few questions of her own.

Rosie smiled and said, "Hello Bob, so you're part of the kidnapping of my granddaughter?"

With a disgusting smile on his face and then laughing at her question, the handcuffed security guard said, "Screw you bitch, I don't have to tell you anything."

Rosie said, "No you don't ass wipe," as she planted the tip of her right foot firmly into the groin of the arrogant man.

As he crumbled to his knees and tears fell like rain from his unbelieving eyes, Rosie smacked the baseball cap off his head and said, "Lets try it again dick head."

Tony saw what was happening and jumped between Rosie and the now crying man.

Rosie said, "Back away Tony, I have more questions for him."

"Rosie, he has rights, you can't do that."

"Whose side are you on Tony? He knows where my granddaughter is."

As Tony tried to calm Rosie down and move her away from Robert Doyle, Juanita lunged at the suspect and dug her nails into the sides of his face screaming, "Where is my daughter you devil?"

Yelling, Robert Doyle said, "Get her off of me."

Having to now pull Juanita off Doyle, Tony said, "Please Rosie, Juanita, we need to act like professionals here or this guy could walk."

Rosie yelled, "WALK, give me five more minutes, and I'll make sure this bastard can't crawl. He knows where my granddaughter is Tony. Don't you understand?"

Pulling Rosie aside, Tony continued, "Sweetheart, this scum can provide us with the information we need to find Lisa but if you abuse him to the point of violating his rights, a good lawyer can clam him up for good."

With Rosie agreeing to keep her hands off and Juanita standing off to the side crying like a baby, Tony helped Bob Doyle to his feet just before the local police chief showed up. First showing the chief his ID, then explaining all the details the best he could in a short time, Tony then provided the chief with his supervisor's name in New York.

Based on the facts supplied by Agent Servantes, the Deputy accompanying the chief read Doyle his rights and placed him in the patrol car.

Bob Doyle, even at that point facing arrest and incarceration, couldn't keep his mouth shut. He yelled, "You'll never see your granddaughter again you bitch."

Tony said, "Help yourself Bob. What else can you tell us?"

But Bob decided he had said enough already, putting his foot in his mouth with that outrage.

The Deputy accompanied by Tony, Rosie, Juanita and Sandy followed in a second patrol car headed for the LaSalle, IL police station.

Agent Jankowski was contacted, who in turn put them in touch with Bud Shari from the Chicago branch of the FBI.

LaSalle chief of police Chester Evans was instructed to hold Doyle, and that the agent would be there first thing in the morning for questioning.

Doyle, who had refused to say anymore after questioning by the chief, was read his rights and placed in a cell for the night.

Rosie, Tony, Juanita and Sandy were given a ride back to the motel, and told they would be contacted in the morning once the agent arrived.

Deciding it was time to check out the accommodations at the motel before going to the local diner for dinner, the three friends walked arm-and-arm to rooms 23 and 24.

Both rooms were furnished alike, but had a different color scheme. There was a queen size bed, TV, dresser, nightstand and a very small bathroom. The thought struck them all at the same time. They had to return to the repair shop and pick up clothes and the necessary essentials that were in the motor home.

Locking the rooms and heading over to the diner first, they had just sat down when Tony's cell phone started ringing, and from the number on the phone he could see that his supervisor was the one calling.

"Agent Servantes, this is Bureau Chief Wallace, I have some information for you on Brian Doyle."

After Tony informed him of the new turn of events, he said, "Chief, I appreciate the call, what have you got on him?"

"First, Brian Doyle has been eluding the authorities for some time, changing his name like some people change their minds. He has four children, two boys and two girls, the oldest being a daughter 42 living in Canada and the youngest the other daughter 36 living in Montana. The two boys, Robert 39 who is a registered and bonded security guard with the hospital in Toledo and Richard 40 who has disappeared. The boys resemble each other so much they could be twins."

"Sounds like a nice compact family sir."

"Richard Doyle has a very colored past with arrests for drug abuse, armed robbery, assault and battery and witness intimidation. He is currently wanted for questioning in the disappearance of a federal informant."

"You didn't mention a mother in all of this?"

"The mother, Vera Fulton Doyle, passed away four years after her last child was born from a kidney infection and was buried in Montana five miles outside of Butte."

"Sir, is there any information on the woman traveling with Brian Doyle?"

"Yes Servantes, her name is Sophie Paxton. At least that's the name she has been using since the divorce from her third husband."

Tony asked, "Three husbands. So where does Doyle fit in?"

"Doyle is just one of her stooges who has been at her side for the past few years, hoping I think to become husband number four."

"What were the other names Paxton went by sir?"

"Her maiden name was Cotter. Her first husband was Alex Taylor and the second husband was Daniel Stark. The third and last that we know about was Steve Paxton."

As the supervisor spoke, Agent Servantes took notes while Rosie and Juanita sat patiently. Before Tony finished his call with his supervisor, he could see that another call was coming in from the local police chief.

"Excuse me sir, I have a call coming in from the local PD, hold on please."

As Tony answered the chief's call, the waitress came to the table and asked, "What can I get you folks?"

Rosie said, "Hold on dear, we'll be with you in a minute, just bring us coffee for now."

"Agent Servantes here, what can I do for you chief?"

"Agent Servantes, I need you to come over to the station and fill out some papers and answer a few questions for me concerning this Doyle character."

"We were just sitting down for dinner chief, but we can be there in an hour if we can get a ride."

"The chief said, "That's fine. Tell Charlie at the garage I said to loan you a car for a couple of days. Meanwhile I'm going to take prints and run a check on the suspect and I'll see you in an hour. Enjoy your dinner."

Getting back with his supervisor, Tony said, "The local chief wants to see me in an hour. He is running a check on Robert Doyle as we speak and will have any additional information for me after dinner."

"Keep me informed Servantes."

"Sir, I hate to ask. What's happening with the Director?"

"For now Servantes, I'm taking the heat and keeping him off your back. I don't know how long I can keep him off you. Don't let me down. Goodbye."

"Goodbye Sir, and thank you."

Looking at his notes and passing on the information to Rosie, Tony said, "The Chief wants to see us at the police station in an hour."

"Are you in trouble Tony with your Director?"

"No, my supervisor is doing a good job keeping him off my back, so far."

Studying the information that Tony had passed on to her, Rosie sat quietly as she went over the names feeling that there might be some connection to her past but she saw nothing that jumped out at her.

30

Finishing a light dinner and discussing the happenings of the day, the tired threesome headed for the repair shop to pick up a few articles of clothing and other needed things. The repair shop owner told Rosie he was happy to do his friend Chief Evans a favor and supply them with a loaner car. He said, "I just happen to have an old Chevy Station Wagon that's sitting around that I can let you use."

After dropping off their belongings at the motel they hurried to the police station to talk with Chief Evans. Not knowing very much about the man they had in custody, Tony and Rosie filled in the chief of police with everything that had happened to that point.

The time was 6:15PM, and in the short time Robert Doyle was in custody, much was revealed about him that he had tried to keep secret. First and most important was that Robert Doyle was in fact Richard Doyle. This was proven by fingerprints that were sent off to the FBI and returned in lightning speed with the assistance of Bureau Chief Wallace, Tony's boss.

Robert's whereabouts were still unknown and Richard would not cooperate with the police at all. Richard knew he had many warrants for his arrest that were outstanding and wanted to negotiate a deal.

The previous married names of Miss Paxton were still circling around in Rosie's memory and for some reason gave her an uncomfortable feeling.

Once it was realized that the man they had in custody was wanted for many crimes, he was removed from the minimum-security cell and placed in maximum-security section.

The FBI would be taking charge of the suspect within the hour and they would be resuming their search for the brother, Robert Doyle.

Meanwhile Rosie, Juanita and Tony were stuck in town until the motor home repairs could be completed.

Rosie told Tony, "I have a plan that might get us out of here sooner but I have to talk with the repair shop owner first."

Rosie's plan was to offer much more money than the repairs had been estimated and Rosie knew that cash, a whole shit load of cash makes things happen.

When Rosie arrived back at the repair shop the owner told her it was her lucky day. The parts driver had just returned with a pair of rebuilt heads, gaskets, hoses and a new water pump. But they were getting ready to quit for the day. Talking with the shop owner and explaining the urgency of getting back on the road she offered him five hundred dollars more then the original estimate.

She told him, "I'll pay you extra if your man will work into the night and get the motor home ready for tomorrow instead of the following day."

He said, "Let me get this right. Instead of the two additional days needed to complete the job, you'll pay me five-hundred on top of my estimate?"

Rosie fanned out five new one-hundred dollar bills and asked, "What do you think Charlie? The original invoice price goes on my Master Card, and these little babies go straight into your pocket."

The mechanic working on the motor home was offered half of the money by his boss, to stay that night and complete the repairs. His answer was, "Let me get something to eat, and put on a pot of coffee and you got a deal boss."

Considering the pay scale in that location, the extra money was more then the mechanic would normally clear for the whole week, and that's what Rosie was counting on.

Rosie returned to the motel and informed Tony and Juanita about her plan to get out of town in the morning, if everything went according to plan.

Deciding to go out to the local Dairy Queen for some late night treats, they would then turn in for the night. What they all needed was a good night's sleep, knowing that they had a long road ahead of them. Rosie knew with a little luck and hard work by the mechanic, and if everything fell into place they could all be leaving a little after sunrise.

31

The sun was coming up behind them as the old green Buick Roadmaster rolled along on I-80 as it was approaching Des Moines, Iowa. A faint knocking sound from the engine that was first noticed about a hundred miles earlier had gotten more pronounced and Doyle noticed a severe drop in the engine oil pressure.

Exiting the I-80 and heading for the town of Norwalk, just a couple miles south of Des Moines, the old Buick's engine problems got so severe the engine quit running and left them stranded on the side of the road.

Miss Paxton and the two children remained in the vehicle as Brian Doyle walked ahead about a quarter mile to a service station that had just opened.

The mechanic at the station drove Doyle back to his car and hooked it up then towed the vehicle back to the shop. It took very little time for the mechanic to determine that the engine was done for and would have to be replaced. After hearing how long it would take, if they were fortunate enough to find a replacement engine at a reasonable cost, it was reluctantly decided by Brian to junk his beautiful car and try to purchase one a little newer from a nearby car lot.

It was not a decision that came easy for Brian because of his love for that old green car, but it was the wisest decision that he could make.

Miss Paxton, who told him, "Brian, if you get rid of this old piece of shit, I'll buy you something newer and better."

Although he was not happy about it, he agreed.

Miss Paxton, who was in sound condition financially, provided Brian with the funds to purchase a five year old Chevy Suburban. The vehicle was in very good condition and more than adequate to handle all their belongings and take them to their final destination. Being a light tan in color Miss Paxton felt the Suburban would not attract very much attention as they continued on their journey.

Since Miss Paxton supplied him with cash obtained from a local bank, Brian was able to buy the vehicle from a private party. This way there was no paper trail to connect him to the purchase.

A few miles out of town, at a shopping mall, Brian pulled up next to a pick-up truck, took out a screwdriver from his jacket pocket and removed the license plates on the pick-up and put them under his seat for possible use at a later date.

With a fresh supply of food, beverages and clean clothes obtained at the market and shopping mall, Miss Paxton told Brian the new direction they would be traveling.

Leaving town the Chevy Suburban headed south on I-35, for the first time changing their westerly direction to south.

Brian Doyle asked, "Just where the hell are we going Miss Paxton? You have kept me in the dark long enough."

"Brian, just follow my directions please. You will know in due time."

Miss Paxton found herself becoming more and more dissatisfied with her companion Brian's lack of obedience. As she explained to him how important it was for him to obey her instructions, he sat in complete disbelief as she rambled on.

The two young children seated in the rear had, over the long trip, seemed to become very passive and were now appearing to accept their captors as the new way of life. The children had no idea that their food had constantly been tainted with drugs to keep them in a passive state of mind.

Brian Doyle had noticed that he had not heard anything from his son Richard, so at the first stop for gas he decided to try calling him. That first stop came in the way of Kansas City, Missouri, and when the concerned Mr. Doyle tried to call his son, the only thing he got was his voicemail advising to leave a message.

The only message the senior Doyle left was, "Call your Dad, there has been a change in plans."

32

Not being able to sleep with all the tossing and turning of Juanita, who was lying next to her in bed, Rosie got up and walked outside with Sandy. It was obvious that the dog appreciated it very much and left a little pile and a few wet puddles around the side of the building. As Rosie walked around slowly breathing in the night's cool clean air, she gave thought to what her next moves would be. She knew they had been getting close to the kidnappers and now fell a couple of days back in her pursuit.

Rosie was never much of a religious person, although her parents were very strict Catholics. On this night with no one but Sandy to hear, Rosie looked up at the sky, clasped her hands together, and said a prayer for her granddaughter's safe return.

Returning to the motel room, she sat down on the one comfortable chair in the room and fell fast asleep. At 8AM the next morning, Rosie was knocking on the door of the repair garage trying to wake up the mechanic who decided to catch a few winks in the front office.

Stumbling to the door, the half sleeping, half awake, mechanic was mumbling out the words, "Alright, alright, I'm coming, hold your horses."

The mechanic, still in his dirty coveralls, no sooner opened the door than Rosie got right into his face, "What the hell are you doing sleeping, you're supposed to be working on my motor home?"

The mechanic smiled, rubbed his face with his hand and told her, "It's all done ma'am. We finished around 5AM, and it runs great. With no other damage found, we finished ahead of schedule."

"Why the hell didn't you call me? I would have been here at six with the rest of the cash."

"I just wanted to give it one test drive before I gave it back to you, but I was too tired, and decided to wait until the sun came up and I rested up a little."

"Well you could have called me."

"Sorry ma'am. Not used to working these kinds of hours."

"Where's your boss?"

"He won't be here until later, but he did the bill for you. It's on the desk, but wait until I get back from my test drive."

As the mechanic took off on his test drive of the now purring motor home, Rosie looked over the itemized repair invoice and was shocked to see the total, but only for a few minutes as she thought about what had been done.

Sitting at the desk looking like she belonged there, a customer came in who wanted an estimate on a tune up. Rosie held up her invoice, pointed at the total and said, "I just came in for an oil change and look what it cost me."

The man, not thinking she was very funny asked, "Looks like you got a good lube job too."

Returning from the test drive with a big smile on his face, the mechanic informed Rosie that all was well and after he cleaned a few fingerprints and smudges off the bumper and hood, it was ready to go.

Rosie asked, "Why doesn't this bill include the extra $500.00 for staying last night?"

The mechanic said, "Can't do that ma'am. That invoice is just for parts and labor. The five hundred dollars bonus you said would be in cash, so that's separate according to the boss."

Not knowing how expensive the same repairs would have cost her back home, Rosie decided to check with Tony and at the same time let Juanita and him know that they would soon be back on the road.

After looking over the repair invoice and calling his mechanic back in New York, Tony told Rosie, "Sweetheart, the same job would have cost you twice as much back in the city. Pay the man and let's get the hell out of here."

Rosie had gone to the local bank the day before and had cashed a check for the estimated amount of repairs. She also got spending money and the extra $500.00 for the mechanic but decided to pay the main repair with a credit card.

After taking care of the motel bill, it took everyone all of an hour to put all of their belongings back in the motor home and get back on the highway heading west. In just three hours, Rosie was pulling into a gas station in Davenport, Indiana to fill up and make a decision whether to continue on the same westerly course or to change plans and head for Nevada.

The FBI had stepped up their investigation having local enforcement agencies set up spot checks along the last known route the kidnappers were taking, that being I-80 west.

Not knowing that the old Buick had been replaced by the newer Chevy Suburban, the kidnappers could have driven right through the check points unnoticed.

Rosie had no way of knowing that the suspects were now headed in a southern direction. So far it looked like they were still on course for Montana.

Making the decision to continue heading west on I-80, the next stop the motor home would make would be in Des Moines to gas up again and check everything under the hood as a precaution. Tony continued to make his calls to his office checking in occasionally for an update on possible spotting of the kidnappers.

After a quick fill up at the gas station and check of all the fluids under the hood, they were on their way to Omaha, Nebraska.

At 4:45PM, the motor home pulled into a 76 gas station in Omaha and all the occupants were ready for a quick stretch of their legs before deciding what to do next.

Rosie confided in Tony that she was feeling lost, not knowing if they were headed in the right direction and whether they should continue towards Montana any longer.

Talking it over between them, it was decided to spend the night in Omaha and think over their decision on traveling west to Montana or southwest to Nevada.

Sitting in a truck stop and studying the detailed map in front of him, Tony said, "Rosie, it's time to make a big decision. If we are going to Billings, Montana, we need to head north on I-29, which will take us to I-90 into Montana. If we stay on I-80, we can go straight into Denver, Colorado, using I-76 from Julesburg. From Denver we take the I-70 to I-15 all the way into Nevada and make our way to Pahrump.

Rosie laughed and said, "Holy shit Tony, you sound like you swallow a friggin map book?"

Tony also laughed and told her, "No sweetheart, with all my advanced training, I was just following the dotted lines."

Rosie stared at him with a lost look in her eyes and for the first time since leaving New York, she wasn't sure which direction to take. Knowing that this decision could take them far out of their way and lose precious time, she asked, "What do you think Tony? Which direction will they go?"

"Sweetheart, it could be a toss of a coin, but just the fact that you mentioned Billings, Montana to him and he just laughed, makes me think that Nevada is where they're headed."

"If you were making the decision, is that the way you would go, Tony?"

"Let's wait until we get some feedback from the Bureau in the morning. They're doing some leg work in both locations and I got a promise that they would let us know the findings."

Rosie, sounding a little tired said, "Okay, let's find a nice motel and check in for the night."

Tony smiled and asked, "That's not usually the way women seduce me. Don't I get a few drinks before you try to get me into your bed?"

Rosie smiled and gave him the finger.

33

With the time difference the way it was, Tony felt he should have heard something by 8AM, but no call had come from the Bureau. Walking outside and finding a comfortable place to sit, he took out his cell phone and called his home office.

Showing his anger to his supervisor after he was informed that there was no new information available was a mistake on his part. Tony was reprimanded and it was made clear once again to him that he was supposedly on vacation and not working in any official capacity.

Bureau Chief Wallace made a strong point of telling Agent Servantes, "You will not call this office and use it as your personal information center. If this office has any information concerning the kidnappers, Miss Castro will be contacted. Is that clear, Agent Servantes?"

Tony took a deep breath and said, "Yes sir. I understand completely."

Rosie had walked up to Tony while he was on the phone and heard most of the call from his side.

She asked, "Any new news Hon?"

He shook his head and said, "Nothing new, and I just got my ass chewed out by my boss. All we can do for now is sit and wait to hear from them."

It was 1 PM of the next day, more than thirty hours had passed and not a word had come from the FBI. Going out walking trying to take their mind off the problem at hand, Rosie, Juanita and Tony were starting to get on each other's nerves.

After Tony's second call in to his supervisor, he was told again, there would not be a need for him to call again. He was told, "There is something new that is being checked so just sit tight, give me one more hour and I'll notify you when it is confirmed."

Agent Wallace also said, "Look Servantes, I know you're very close to the Castro family. I don't mean to be a hard ass but I have to follow proper procedure. I'll call you in a little while, hopefully."

Tony said, "Thank you boss. I'll pass on the information to Miss Castro."

Even after hearing the news from Tony, Rosie lost it. She told him, "Your Supervisor can be a real idiot at times. I'll give him one more hour Tony, and then we're leaving for Nevada whether we hear from him or not."

Reluctantly Tony agreed and after the hour passed they were making their way to the Interstate. It would probably be another twenty-four hours before they reached Pahrump, Nevada and then the task would be to be as discreet as possible, so as not to warn the kidnappers while they searched the area.

Juanita had taken to a habit of uncontrollable crying sessions and Rosie's nerves were raw as could be. Rosie had driven in heavy traffic over six and a half hours and told Tony, "I'm going to stop for coffee and something to eat, and maybe stretch my legs a little."

The turnoff ahead was for a town called Gothenburg. So looking for a place to gas up and grab a snack and coffee was the first thing on Rosie's mind. Spotting a nice looking family type restaurant just up the road from the Interstate exit, Tony said, "That looks like a good place to stop."

It was around 9 PM, so it wasn't too busy at the 24 hour restaurant/ truck stop/ motel.

The parking area was behind the buildings and because of the late hour and the available overnight parking for truckers, it wasn't a surprise to see a dozen or more big rigs lined up and engines shut off. Before anyone had a chance to open the door of the motor home, Sandy was sitting there waiting to get out and find a nice place to relieve herself.

As Tony and Juanita walked to the rear entrance of the diner, Rosie walked Sandy around the brightly lit parking lot, all the time aware of her surroundings.

Walking into the restaurant, it was obvious that the owner cared very much about first impressions presented to customers. The walls were knotty pine, not paneling, but the real tongue and grove expensive boards. The carpeting was a light gray with a swirling line pattern, very clean looking with no visible wear from foot traffic. The booths that were along the wall on the left side were upholstered in a soft warm red material, looking very inviting to sit on.

Four customers were seated at the counter watching a hanging TV that was mounted near a door that looked like it led to the kitchen. The men never even glanced in Tony and Juanita's direction. Their eyes seemed to be glued to the TV.

From behind the all white Formica counter, backed by all stainless steel appliances, a soft spoken woman in her mid fifties greeted the couple and said, "I'll be with you in a second folks. Have a seat wherever you feel comfortable."

Before the waitress returned, Rosie had come in and sat down next to Juanita and said, "Nice choice Tony."

With a big smile on her face and three menus in her hand the waitress said, "Hi folks, my name is Veronica, can I get you something to drink while you look over the menu?"

Tony was the first to speak, "Hi dear, coffees all around and a few minutes to see what else you have."

Rosie asked where the restrooms were and she and Juanita took a little walk to freshen up. Tony also got up from the booth and walked over to a rack that held the local newspaper and a couple of magazines. When the ladies returned to the table, the waitress brought the coffees and glasses of water and said, "I'll give you a few more minutes to decide."

Rosie and Juanita both ordered breakfast meals while Tony went for a burger and fries.

After a few cups of coffee and a well deserved rest in the comfortable surrounding, Tony ask the waitress for the check and also asked her how far it was to the Colorado state line.

"Hon, you have about ninety miles, then watch for the I-76 and that will take you straight into Denver, if that's where you folks are headed."

Rosie asked, "Just by chance Veronica, you don't remember seeing an older couple with two young girls stopping in here in the past week, do you?"

"No, sorry dear I don't. Listen, you folks have a nice trip."

Leaving the restaurant and walking slowly to the motor home, Tony said, "How about spending the night here, and getting a fresh start in the morning? I know we haven't been on the road that long today, but a little more rest would do us all some good."

Rosie said, "You know Tony, I was just thinking the same thing. A good night's sleep would sure feel nice. My back is starting to tighten up."

As Juanita walked back to the motor home, Tony and Rosie went for a walk across the road and along a row of stores that were closed for the night. Sharing some warm feelings and even for just a few minutes forgetting what their mission was, Rosie squeezed Tony's hand so slightly and said, "Tony, I'm so happy you're here. This would have been so tough without you."

Tony smiled and said, "Sweetheart, maybe one day when this is all over and Lisa is back home where she belongs, we can talk a little about us and our future together."

Rosie held Tony's hand and said, "Hon, you know I love you dearly. You and I have always been close but I don't know if I'm ready to let someone in on a full time basis. Maybe one day I'll know, but until then no one has a better place in my heart than you."

Kissing him on the cheek, she said, "Let's get some sleep Hon, tomorrow's going to be a busy day."

As they walked back to the parking lot they continued holding hands. What she had just told Tony was true in every way, except she had always looked at Tony as a big brother but never as a love interest.

34

Miss Sophie Paxton lost her right leg just below the knee approximately ten years earlier from diabetes and she has never accepted the fact that giving up her leg saved her life. Over the years she has developed a strong hatred for doctors, especially the rich and famous ones.

Sitting in the car riding with her companion Brian Doyle, she has made it a daily habit of reminding him how uncomfortable she was. She keeps telling him that she has developed a severe pain just above the right knee and has chewed him out for not letting her visit a specialist in Chicago.

While Brian was fueling the Suburban up as they sat at a gas station in Grand Junction, Colorado, Miss Paxton walked to the restroom. As she was returning to the vehicle, she let out a loud scream and started limping. The scream was so loud that it attracted the attention of several other customers who were filling their tanks or just walking by.

Falling to the ground, Miss Paxton struggled and tried to remove her prosthetic leg so she could alleviate the pain. Several people came to her aide but she just chased them away, telling them all, "Just get the hell away from me."

Brian Doyle had heard the scream and quickly came to her aide, but the arrogant woman just yelled, "You too, get away from me you fool."

The artificial leg had a clamping device and a pocket that was cushioned by foam padding that Miss Paxton had installed herself several weeks before. The problem was not in the foam but from a wire that was used to construct the cup portion molded from fiberglass. The cup had cracked, probably from faulty materials or being mistreated by the woman it was attached to.

In either case, Brian would have to assist her back into the vehicle and they would have to locate a facility that could make the repairs needed very soon or they would be in big trouble.

Carefully lifting the woman up onto her good leg, Brian then had her put her arm around him and they slowly walked back to their vehicle.

Calling a local hospital, Miss Paxton was told that the most likely place for repairs or replacement of her equipment would be in the city of Denver. Unfortunately for them they had driven through Denver a few hours earlier which meant backtracking approximately 200 miles.

The second option was to wait until they arrived in Las Vegas, which lay approximately 350 miles ahead and then only 50 more miles to Pahrump.

Miss Paxton was very familiar with the facility in Denver. It had provided her with her prosthetic leg years earlier and she didn't mind backtracking to the familiar surroundings.

Brian, on the other hand, was very upset with the idea of turning around and heading back to a hospital in Denver. He told her, "Why should we drive all the way back to Denver when a hospital in Las Vegas can provide you with the same replacement or repair?"

As Brian voiced his opinion, he was told, "Brian, you turn this fucking car around, or get the hell out and I will find someone else to drive me there."

Not liking what he had just been told, he voiced his opinion once again, but this time with much anger in his voice. "Sophie, I put up with so much of your abuse, and I don't deserve it, so please back off. We're going to Denver, just as you requested. But I'm warning you, I will not stand for much more of your abusive treatment."

"Just get us there as fast as you can."

Three and a half hours later they arrived back in Denver at the hospital Miss Paxton insisted on going too, and Brian had nothing more to say.

Not far behind, the motor home with Rosie, Juanita, and Tony was making up ground, but they had no idea how really close they were once again.

35

Rosie had been driving along at 70 miles per hour, on I-76, since getting on the road at 6 AM that morning. They were about one hour outside of Denver at 11AM, when Tony's cell phone started buzzing away.

Tony's Bureau Chief, Al Wallace, was calling back finally with information concerning the deceased girl in the hospital in Toledo. Also, the suspicions were correct on the direction the kidnappers were headed. It had been revealed through extensive questioning of an associate of Brian Doyle's in Montana that Pahrump was Doyle's final destination.

Agent Wallace said, "Through many hours of interrogation and a little bit of deal making with

Richard Doyle, he revealed that he had switched identities with his brother Robert. The location on the real Robert Doyle is still not available but a pick-up for questioning warrant has been issued.

The identity tag, papers, and information on the deceased little girl in the hospital was done to confuse the FBI investigation. Richard Doyle also intentionally switched paper work, tags and information on over twenty other bodies in the hospital morgue to cause mass confusion."

Tony asked, "Tell me about the dead child?"

"The little girl was and is a Jane Doe, discovered in a vacant lot just outside of town and has still not been identified"

Tony responded with, "Holy shit Chief. That son of a bitch is just as sick as his father."

Agent Wallace went on, "Since the discovery of all the misidentified corpses, switched paper work, ID tags and bracelets, the hospital and staff have been under investigation by the FBI and the State Attorney General's Office."

Rosie asked, "What's going on Tony?"

"It's my Supervisor. Rosie give me a few minutes please and I'll fill you in."

Rosie frantically asked, "Is it Lisa?"

Tony said, "No. Just hold on Rosie and I'll tell you when I get off the phone."

"Ok Chief, what else you got?"

"That's it for now Servantes. Where are you?"

Tony said, "Just outside of Denver Chief."

"Servantes, I just hope for your sake that your personal involvement doesn't get you in over your head because I won't be able to help you."

"It's way past that Chief, these people are like family to me and I'm in it until the end. If I need to, I want to change this vacation to temporary reassignment to the Las Vegas office. "

"Don't step over the line Servantes, don't step over the line. Are you sure that's what you want?"

"Look Chief, if that will take the heat off of you, just make it happen."

"I'll call you if that's the way it goes."

"You know where to find me Chief."

"Yes I do. Good bye."

"I'll stay in touch Chief, good bye."

Rosie asked, "What was that about?"

After going over everything with Rosie that his supervisor had told him, it was time to get back to their original plans.

Juanita was seated at the table writing a letter to her friend back in New York while Tony went into the bathroom to shave, getting rid of a couple of days of growth.

The sun was high in the clear sky and was reflecting off signs warning of animal crossings. Rosie was describing a complete steak lunch that she would like to have when they arrived in Denver, but no one was listening to her. Suddenly a deer ran across the highway and although she tried very hard to avoid hitting the animal, it was not to be. The loud thump followed by the motor home swerving side to side got everyone's attention.

Juanita yelled, "Mom, what was that?"

"We just hit a deer Hon. I need to pull over somewhere."

Finding a safe place where the shoulder was wide enough for the motor home, Rosie stopped and then backed up so they were directly across from the deer. Once they all got out of the vehicle, the first thing they checked the animal.

It appeared that the deer had died on impact and the motor home had sustained massive body damage including a cracked windshield.

A witness to the accident who followed only a short distance behind the motor home happened to work at the local sheriff's department and was on her way into work to start her shift. She called the report in to her office so a patrol car could be dispatched immediately. Several other motorists also pulled over to the side of the road to see if they could offer any assistance.

When Rosie checked out the motor home after seeing that there was nothing they could do for the deer, she took one look at the front of the vehicle, turned around and said, "AH SHIT, this is going to slow us up for a long time."

There was blood everywhere, and the carcass of the animal was lying off to the side of the road. When Juanita looked closely at the deer, she said, "Oh mom, that poor animal."

A patrol car from the sheriff's department at Fort Morgan arrived on the scene in just a few minutes, with a paramedic's unit and animal control right behind it.

Rosie's response to the attention paid to a deer's tragic death and vehicle damage was, "Back in the city it would take a very high profile crime to warrant this kind of quick response, but I'm thankful for it."

It was decided that it would be better if the motor home was towed into town and checked out by a body shop and mechanic before continuing on the trip west. While sitting and waiting for the tow truck to arrive, Tony received another call from his bureau office in New York but this time his supervisor was not as friendly. The information Servantes received this time was a conformation of what his supervisor had told him earlier, with some additional news that filled in many of the blanks.

Through extensive questioning of friends and family of the Doyles in Montana, it was confirmed that the kidnappers had no intention of returning to that state.

One friend of Brian Doyle's insisted he talked with Doyle and he was told he would be returning to Montana. After hard questioning and the threat of incarceration, he admitted it was all a lie to throw the authorities off Doyle's track.

Checking through state records in Nevada, it was found out that Miss Paxton owned several large parcels of land in Pahrump and in the Reno area. So it seemed more likely that one of those areas would be their final destination.

Also, many years earlier when Miss Paxton was married to a man named Edward Stark she had a son named Lester. While investigating the background of the Stark family, it was discovered that the man who shot Rosie Castro in that tenement building was named Lester Stark. Detective Castro was the officer who shot and killed Stark while she was serving with the Newark Police Department back in New Jersey.

This fact seemed to put an answer to the question of why Rosie's granddaughter was kidnapped, and why they keep referring to her as Detective Castro.

Chief Al Wallace said, "Agent Servantes, you are ordered to cease your part in the manhunt for the kidnappers, and return to this office in New York, immediately."

Without hesitation, Tony said, "Excuse me sir, but I am still on vacation."

"Agent Servantes, you have been working on tracking down those kidnappers, and you are way outside of our jurisdiction. I have given you a lot of leeway because the parent of the child is a friend of yours. You are way too close to the situation for you to go on. It cannot be overlooked any longer. You are hereby ordered to return to New York immediately."

"Sir, no disrespect meant, but I am on vacation. I am not using the fact that I am an agent with the FBI to persuade or push anyone into cooperating with Miss Castro. She is a private citizen who has the right to look for her missing granddaughter. So I ask that you reconsider your request."

"Servantes, it is not a request. It is an order for your return to New York and it comes from a higher authority. I am just following orders and so will you. Get on a plane and get back here now."

"Yes Sir, I'll try to be there as soon as I can make the arrangements."

Rosie heard the last part of the conversation and asked, "You'll be where when you make what arrangements?"

"Sorry Hon, I need to find an airport and get my ass back to New York. It's Bureau orders."

"What the hell is that all about Tony?"

"The orders came from up above and I can't disregard them without getting my ass in a lot of trouble."

"I understand Tony. You know Juanita and I are going to miss you."

Tony said, "First I need to tell you some new information. Does the name Lester Stark stand out in your memory?"

Rosie answered, "Of course. He's the bastard who shot me years ago and screwed up my life."

"Well, prepare yourself. The woman in the car that we are chasing is... was... his mother."

Rosie just stood there a couple of minutes and had to digest what she had just heard.

Juanita, who had taken Sandy for a walk while things were being discussed with the officer and the other people who had shown up at the scene, returned just in time to hear Tony say that he was going back to New York.

With tears in her eyes Juanita asked, "Tony, why are you leaving us? We need you?"

"Sweetheart, it's orders from my boss and I can't disobey, I must leave."

Waiting to tell Juanita about the new information, Rosie asked the officer, "Sergeant, where is the closest airport?"

"The Fort Morgan Municipal Airport is just a short drive from here on Highway 52."

"Would you drop my friend here at the airport after the tow truck comes and hooks us up?"

"Sorry ma'am, I'm not a taxi service."

Tony took out his ID, showed it to the officer and asked, "How about a little professional courtesy Sergeant?"

Smiling and folding his arms on his chest, the sergeant said, "I think I can make an exception in your case Agent Servantes."

As Tony went back into the motor home to pack up his belongings, Rosie followed right behind him. She asked him if there was anything else he knew about the kidnappers.

When he turned to talk to her he told her no, and apologized for having to leave her. She hugged him then looked him in the eyes and said, "I love you my dear friend, and I know you would stay if you could, but we'll be okay I promise."

"Rosie, I'm going to call you every day and I don't want any bullshit from you, just the truth. Watch out for these people. They are dangerous nuts and I wouldn't put anything past them. Be careful."

"I will, I promise, and I'll keep in touch with you."

Tony looked in Rosie's eyes and saw the tears welling up and gently kissed her on the cheek.

She hugged him and said, "Goodbye Tony, thank you for all your help."

A knock on the door and the words from the officer came, "Tow truck is here ma'am."

As the driver hooked up, Rosie exited the motor home and watched Tony as he drove away in the patrol car.

36

The sun appeared to be directly overhead, as in high noon, and Tony was comfortably flying back to the east coast. Rosie and Juanita were sitting in a Denny's restaurant sipping coffee waiting for the report on the condition of the motor home.

As they sat there, Rosie told Juanita about the connection of the kidnappers and the shooting years ago, and said, "I'm so sorry sweetheart that my past has caused all this hurt for you and Lisa."

Reaching across the table, Juanita held her mom's hand. "Mom it's not your fault, those people are just evil."

Staring out of the large picture window next to their booth, Rosie mumbled the words, "Why the hell are all these things happening to us to slow us down?"

Juanita said, "Mom we'll catch them, I'm so sure now, and I know you are too."

"Hon, first there's the shooting of that asshole, slowing us down. Then there was the engine trouble. And now a friggin deer jumps in front of the motor home. On top of all of it, Tony gets called back to New York. Damn, I'm going to miss him."

"Mom, you didn't want him to join us at first when he showed up unexpectedly."

"Things change sweetheart. It was that added feeling of security that I'll miss."

Just then, Rosie's cell phone started playing a new song that Tony had programmed on her phone. "I Can See Clearly Now, The Rain Has Gone."

Rosie looked at her phone and said, "What the hell? Who the hell did that to my phone?"

Meanwhile it kept playing it over and over, "I Can See Clearly Now, The Rain Has Gone."

Answering, Rosie looked at Juanita and said, "That's got to change."

The call was from the shop down the street, letting her know that there was no mechanical damage to the vehicle, only body damage and it was safe to drive.

Leaving Denny's, Juanita said, "They haven't stopped us yet mom. Just like you've said all along, we will find them, and I believe you."

Rosie hugged her daughter and for the first time looked at her in a different light, seeing how much stronger she had become.

They walked arm in arm back to the motor home and as they got closer, Sandy, who was tied up next to the building, barked and jumped, stretching the rope to its extreme, almost breaking it.

Rosie had wrapped up a few pieces of bacon for their loyal canine companion. With her nose sniffing at the air as her welcomed masters returned, Sandy jumped, smacked her lips and even howled a little until she received her bacon reward.

After taking care of the bill, Rosie, Juanita and Sandy found their way back to the interstate and continued on the trip west.

The shop owner had washed away the blood from the front of the vehicle, replaced the windshield and knocked out some of the damage to the front. But no matter how much he had done, the memory of hitting that animal was still fresh in Rosie's mind. That collision with one of wildlife's finest showed as she drove at a much slower speed than before.

Juanita had tried to call Tony to let him know that they were back on the road but all she got both times was his voice mail.

Looking closely at her mom's cell phone as she attempted to change the song on it, Juanita noticed a couple of missed calls: one from Tony, the second from an unknown caller.

Sitting in the passenger seat Juanita played Tony's message first. It said, "Hi sweetheart, boarding the plane now, I'll call you when we land."

The second message was, "Hello Detective Castro, can't seem to get a hold of you, but I'll try again later. Enjoy your drive."

37

Sitting in a motel room down the road from the Denver Hospital, where Sophie Paxton was having her prosthetic leg repaired, Brian Doyle sat with his cell phone in his hand having just left a needling message on Rosie's voicemail.

The two young girls sat watching cartoons on the TV in the adjoining room through slightly glazed eyes caused by drugs they were given each day. They were seemingly unaware that almost six weeks had passed since their abduction by the cruel elderly couple with nothing but evil retribution on their minds.

Going over the past weeks in his mind, Brian Doyle's thoughts took him back to living in Toledo, Ohio for almost two of the weeks with his

200

son. There was a horrible week living in Grove City, Pennsylvania, waiting for a mechanic to locate a rear end for his old Buick. There had been almost a full month of sleazy motels, uncomfortable driving conditions and a complaining vindictive woman at his side.

His moments of reliving the past were broken up as he was startled by the ringing of the cell phone still held in his hand.

Sophie Paxton was feeling her oats again. She said, "Brian, put those little brats in the car and come pick me up. Don't waste any time, get your ass here now."

"Yes, Miss Paxton, I'll be there as soon as I can."

She yelled at him, "You get here now, Brian, I'm ready to leave now, do you understand me? I said now."

"Yes Miss Paxton, I understand you."

The phone connection had already been broken, so Brian Doyle just got up from his chair and walked to the room with the kids and said, "Lets go kids, we need to go pick up the 'Wicked Witch of the West'."

It was obvious that he was getting un-enchanted with his abusive companion of many years. He had decided to tolerate her abusive behavior for some reason that was deeply seated in his mind. He felt there was nothing he could do at this stage in their relationship short of shooting her and dumping her body somewhere.

Loading the kids into the Suburban, Doyle headed for the hospital and thought about what their next move might be.

At times he would think about just walking away from the entire situation and just move on with his life. In reality, his mental make-up was short of the average person of his years.

38

As Rosie drove down the highway headed for a town in Nevada, a place she could hardly pronounce called Pahrump, she had one thing on her mind, and that was finding her granddaughter while catching the bastards who kidnapped her.

The depression of Tony leaving was starting to get to her and talking about it to Juanita was not an option in her mind. Rosie would say, "I just don't want to talk about it."

Juanita would become so frustrated. She would just retreat to the bedroom and lie down.

Rosie could feel the pressure mounting, but she tried to keep it under wraps. She knew when the time came to confront the kidnappers she would have to act professionally and not let her emotions run wild.

She became obsessed with getting to Pahrump as soon as possible and she decided to drive straight through. The only stops would be for gas or bathroom breaks, with no more overnight stops for sleeping.

As she pressed on driving on Interstate 70 heading west with Denver in her rear view mirror, she had no idea she had passed the bastards she was seeking.

Stopping for gas in Grand Junction, Colorado, Rosie was hoping that she wouldn't have to stop again for gas until she reached Nevada.

With the motor home traveling over some dangerous roads through the mountain areas, Juanita thought it best to return to the passenger seat and keep her mom company, with or without conversation.

As the hours passed and the Nevada Stateline came into view, Rosie finally broke her silence saying, "It is about time. I never thought we would get here."

Pulling into a gas station in Mesquite, Nevada, Rosie parked next to the gas pump and turned off the motor, looked at Juanita and said, "It won't be long now sweetheart, only about a hundred miles more."

Juanita asked, "Mom, what are we going to do first when we get there?"

"Honey, I've been thinking about that for the past two hundred miles and I think our first stop will be the police station, or the sheriff's department, I don't know what kind of law enforcement they have there, but we are sure going to find out."

"Do you think they are aware of those horrible people who kidnapped Lisa and the other little girl?"

"I don't know Honey, but I have the feeling that Tony may have already called ahead."

"Speaking of Tony mom, how about we give him a call before we get to Pahrump?"

"I'll tell you what, after we gas up, I'll pull over to the side there and we'll have something to eat and give him a call."

"I'd like that mom, I really would."

"Okay, lets do it. But first I have to pee."

39

As Tony sat in the main office of the FBI in New York City, he listened to Agent Robert Stevens summing up his investigation on a weapons smuggling operation, but his thoughts were not in that room at all.

Every other minute Tony's supervisor would look over at him and finally when there was a break in the summary, Bureau Chief Supervisor Al Wallace asked, "Agent Servantes, where is your head at? It sure as hell isn't in this room. Follow me to my office."

As they walked into the Chief's office, he said, "Close the door behind you and sit down."

The Chief said, "Okay Servantes, what's going on?"

"Sir, in all honesty, my thoughts are with two brave women who are trying to locate two scared little girls who were kidnapped by a couple of sick people."

"Agent Servantes, clear your head. That is not our business at hand."

"Excuse me sir, but this was a crime that we have turned our backs on."

"That will be enough Agent Servantes."

"No Sir, that's the problem. We have not done enough. These people need our help and we dropped the ball."

"I said that's enough Servantes. The regional offices out west are investigating and have things under control."

Tony ranted on, "That woman. That ex police detective has done more on this case with little help from us than the whole Bureau put together. She is so close to finding the kidnappers but needs our help now."

"Agent, you need some time off to get your head straight and get back with the program."

"Sir, with all due respect, I was on my goddamn vacation when you called me back in, and you're right, I need to be getting back to it. I should be allowed to spend it where and with whom I choose to spend it."

"Servantes, stay away from that woman. That is an order."

"Sir, I have five weeks vacation time coming. I'll see you when it's over."

"You walk out of here with the intention of sticking your nose back into that kidnapping investigation and your ass is on report, period. You're looking at severe disciplinary actions for insubordination."

"Report me sir, because that's exactly were I'm headed."

"You're on suspension Servantes."

"And you're an ass at times sir. One who is so wrapped up in proper procedure and making himself look good to his supervisors, that you forgot what it's like to be a helping human being."

"I can't afford that luxury Servantes."

"Well maybe it's about time that the Bureau adds a few more chips to the pot, but I'm not waiting for you to decide. I'm on vacation, suspension or not."

"Servantes, the only reason I have given you so much leeway with what you have been doing is my respect for your father."

"Sir, leave my father out of this."

"Your father and I spent twenty-five years working side by side to improve conditions in the bureau. It's only his memory and past friendship that keeps me from booting your ass out."

Tony said, "Sir."

"No Servantes, I don't want to hear anymore from you. You ever talk to me like that again I'll run your ass out of the Bureau so fast it will make your head spin. Now get the hell out of my office and call me with any information you or your lady friend happen on. You're on vacation, I hope you enjoy yourself."

Walking out of the Bureau Chief's office, Tony stopped at the door, turned and said, "Thanks Al, you know I respect what you think."

The chief said, "Get the hell out of here Tony."

Leaving the office, heading to his car in the parking structure, Tony's cell phone started ringing. When he heard the caller's voice he smiled and said, "Hi sweetheart, are you two doing okay?"

"Hi Tony, Mom and I are doing fine. We're in a gas station about a hundred miles from Pahrump. She says we should be there in a couple hours."

"Is your Mom there with you now?

"Yes she is."

"Can I talk to her dear?"

"Sure Tony, here she is."

Rosie said, "Hi Tony, how are things back in the City?"

"Better now that I'm talking with you again."

"We're almost there Tony. Pahrump, we're so close."

"What are your plans Rosie?"

"I plan to visit the Police Department or the Sheriff's Office, whichever law enforcement they have there, first. I was hoping you might have called ahead, but I guess you didn't."

"No I haven't called, but I will. By the way, I believe they have both there, sheriff and police."

"Thank you Tony. I'll let you know how I do with them."

"Keep your cell on you; I'll be calling you back in a little while. Bye doll."

"Bye Tony, talk to you soon."

Tony found the information he was looking for pretty fast and then he called Rosie back.

"That was quick Tony."

"I found out that you need to go to the Nye County Sheriff's Office in Pahrump, I spoke to a deputy who told me Sheriff Norton Majors was the head law enforcement in Pahrump. They have two locations, but I'm sure any one of the locals there can point you in the right direction to the main office."

"Thanks Tony, I'll call and let you know how we make out."

Tony said, "Oh Rosie, by the way. I am back on vacation time as we speak, so how about I join you and Juanita for breakfast tomorrow morning?"

"Ah Tony, that's not necessary."

"It may not be necessary, but it's what I want to do, unless you don't want me there?"

"Want you here? I cried when you left Tony. I miss you so much my friend."

"Rosie, I'll see you in Pahrump in the morning, unless I can't get a flight. Then it will have to be lunch, because I'm on my way."

"We can pick you up at the airport in Las Vegas if it will help?"

"Thanks Rosie, but I'll be flying into Las Vegas and then renting a car at the airport. See you tomorrow in Pahrump, bye."

"Bye Tony, see you tomorrow."

40

Within two hours, Rosie and Juanita were walking into the Nye County Sheriff's Office in Pahrump, Nevada.

Rosie introduced herself and Juanita to the dispatcher and deputy on duty and asked to speak with the Sheriff. The dispatcher informed the sheriff who was seated in his office of their need to talk with him.

A tall man probably in his mid fifties came forward and said, "Hello ladies, my name is Sheriff Majors, how can I help you?"

Rosie filled in the sheriff on her background in law enforcement and said, "Would it be possible to speak in private Sheriff?"

Pointing the way to his office the Sheriff said, "Right this way ladies," but left the door open.

Stepping behind his desk, Sheriff Majors asked, "What can I do for you Miss Castro?"

After explaining partially all that had taken place over the past couple months, Rosie asked if he was familiar with the property owned by a Miss Sophie Paxton.

Sheriff Majors told Rosie, "Ma'am, I'm not familiar with the people or the location of the property you're inquiring about. My suggestion to you is to go to the County Registrar's office. I'm sure they can provide you with the information you are requesting."

Standing up from behind his desk, the Sheriff also told Rosie, "Ma'am, if these people are guilty of what you're telling me, this is a matter for law enforcement, not for a civilian. From what you have told me, you are no longer in law enforcement."

Taking the remark by the Sheriff as calmly as possible, Rosie responded, "Civilian? Sheriff, I had seventeen years working experience in one of the worst crime areas in the country."

"Yes ma'am, but you're retired now, and it's out of your hands. You have no authority here, but I do. So I'm asking you nicely, please let us do our jobs. I promise I will look into your situation if you give me all the information I'll need."

Trying now very hard to control her temper, Rosie told him, "Sheriff, I will take it under advisement. Now can you tell me where I can find the Registrar's Office?"

The Sheriff drew Rosie a small map and gave her the address of the office she needed to go to, and when he handed it to her he said, "Just know Miss Castro, if you interfere with the Sheriff's Department in any way, I will not hesitate to arrest you for obstruction of justice."

Rosie was ready to unload on the Sheriff and Juanita saw it, so she just grabbed her mom's arm and said, "Thank you Sheriff, we promise to stay out of your way," and then she pulled her mom out of the office.

Being that it was already late in the day and the Registrar's office was closed, Rosie walked back into the Sheriff's office and said, "I'm sorry Sheriff, I don't mean to step on your authority, it's just that I know I'm so close. The FBI tells me they had the investigation in full force but I haven't seen it."

"Miss Castro, I'll do what I can to help, but like I said before, I'll check into it and let you know what I find out. Where can I contact you?"

"Well that's something else Sheriff. Where might we be able to park the motor home for the night?"

Once again the Sheriff took out his pad and drew a map where an RV Park was located. It was about a mile from the Sheriff's office.

Thanking the Sheriff, Rosie left his office with a different idea in mind.

Driving down the main road in town, Rosie chose to pull in and park at one of the large food mart stores located on Main Street.

Juanita went into the store to do some shopping for supplies as Rosie sat and contemplated what her next move might be.

As a result of pushing herself to the limits, Rosie was completely exhausted, so when she lay down on the bed hoping to take a short nap before dinner, she slept for six straight hours before waking up to take a bathroom break.

After reading for a while, Juanita chose to sack out on the couch after a quick snack.

The morning seemed to come quick and with the coolness of the morning air, Rosie decided to take a walk and clear her head just after sun up. The walk was helping even if just temporarily, but it helped her concentrate on her plans for that day.

Tony had taken a redeye flight out of Newark Airport in New Jersey and would arrive in Las Vegas before the sun came up and had made plans for a last minute helicopter ride to Pahrump.

With additional information on the kidnappers, he was looking forward to reuniting with Rosie and Juanita.

Although his superiors had taken Tony out of the information loop, he still had his own connections through friends in the bureau and all it took was a couple of phone calls to old friends.

The helicopter ride he had planned on didn't pan out because of mechanical problems, so his next option was a rental car and a forty-five minute drive to Pahrump.

Before leaving the car rental yard, Tony made a call to Rosie to find out where they had parked for the night and made arrangements to meet them when he arrived in town.

Part of the new information Tony had acquired was about the old Buick the kidnappers had been driving but was no longer their means of transportation.

As Tony drove along the main street in Pahrump, it didn't take long for him to spot the food mart where Rosie had parked for the night.

Pulling up next to the motor home, he noticed both women sitting in lawn chairs on the shady side of the vehicle along with Sandy, who was lying comfortably between them.

With smiles on their faces they both remained seated until Tony got out of the car, and then burst into a run to greet him with Sandy barking by their side.

First Juanita hugged Tony and then it was Rosie's turn. She planted a warm affectionate kiss on his cheek as she hugged him saying, "Sweetheart, I'm so glad you're back here. We missed your warm smiling face."

"Hi Rosie, how did you make out with the local law officials. Was there any good news from the Sheriff on the kidnappers?"

"Tony, being that he's not familiar with Sophie Paxton, all he could tell us was that we needed to check with the Registrar's Office to find the location of the property owned by the woman."

Juanita spoke up, "He also told mom he would lock her up if she interfered with the Sheriff's Department's involvement in the kidnapping."

Rosie said, "Yeah, the big jerk. He doesn't know anything about it, but yet tells me to back off."

"I'll have a talk with him sweetheart."

"So you said you had some new information for us. Is it good news?"

Tony sat down on the motor home step and told the women, "They are no longer driving the old Buick Roadmaster. It seems you're not the only one to have vehicle problems. They blew up the engine in Iowa and had to junk the old clunker and pick up something newer."

Rosie asked, "What are they driving now?"

"From what a very smart agent in Iowa found out, they purchased a Chevy Suburban in a town called Norwalk. The old Buick was supposed to be destroyed in a crusher at the junkyard where it was towed, but it wasn't."

Rosie said, "But?"

"But the wrecking yard owner didn't have the heart to destroy the old classic and decided to register and repair it for himself. So he took the papers on the car and went to the local DMV and transferred ownership immediately."

Juanita asked, "So how did you find out so fast?"

"Thank God for the computer age." Rosie said laughing.

"That's it. It threw up a red flag and the FBI was notified immediately. An agent was sent there from a local branch office in Des Moines."

Rosie asked, "So now we're looking for what?"

Tony said, "A Chevy Suburban."

Rosie asked, "You have a description, color and year?"

"From information provided by one of the local banks, the agent was able to contact the previous owner who told him the vehicle is a 1996 light brown Chevy Suburban, license number TLC 233."

"How the hell did they know at the bank who sold that vehicle?"

"Miss Sophie Paxton cashed a bank voucher for $10,000.00 at the B of A Bank in Norwalk. That very afternoon, a cash deposit by Mrs. Mildred Bryant was made into her account and she told the teller about selling her car to a stranger from out of town. The man told her he had to junk his old beautiful Buick at Willis's Wrecking Yard that morning and was in a very solemn mood."

Rosie said, "What a stroke of luck."

Tony smiled and said, "Luck? I'll have you know, that's the way a well-oiled machine works; a great FBI investigation in progress."

"Yeah, and lots of "bullshit luck," but I love it."

"Well, whatever made it happen; at least we have new information on the kidnappers."

41

After picking up the very annoyed Miss Paxton at the Denver Hospital, Brian Doyle found his way back to the interstate and continued to head west.

"Miss Paxton, if we drive straight through, we can be in Nevada by noon tomorrow. How does that sound to you?"

"That would be fine Brian, but with one change."

"What's that ma'am?"

"We're not going to Pahrump."

"Then where may I ask are we going?"

"We're going to Reno, beautiful, beautiful, Reno."

"What the hell are we going to Reno for?"

"You don't ask questions. You just follow orders Brian."

"I'm glad you told me now, before we headed too far southwest. I need to pull over and look at the map before we travel too far out of our way."

"Pull over then and get us headed in the right direction you fool. I want you to find a town called Delta in the western part of Utah. That's where we are going to stay for a couple of weeks before we head for Reno."

After a long stare at the rude and obnoxious woman, Brian Doyle pulled off the first exit ramp to find a safe spot to study the map of the western states and possibly get an explanation for the change of destination.

A tree-lined parking lot with several driveways looked like a perfect spot for Brian to park the Suburban and check the map. Since it was a Sunday morning, the shopping center it was next to was closed.

Looking carefully at the map, Brian spoke up and said, "Good, we can continue on Interstate 70 west until it branches off on Route 50. Then we can take that straight to Delta. Is that okay with you Miss Paxton?"

"Yes that's fine Brian."

"May I ask why we are not going to Pahrump?"

Not liking her decisions questioned but understanding the reason for concern, Sophie Paxton asked, "Do you remember Christina Larsen?"

"Isn't that your niece?"

"Yes Brian, my sister and brother-in-law's kid."

"You mean, Helen and Henry's kid?" Brian asked.

"Yes Brian, the oldest one."

"Well what about her?"

"Just shut up and listen Brian. Christina works at the Sheriff's Dept in Pahrump and she overheard some Latino woman asking questions about me, and my property there. The sheriff told her to check with the county registrar's office for information on property owners. The woman's been asking questions at local stores to find out where I am and who, if anyone has seen me lately."

"Did they tell her anything?"

"They don't know anything you fool. We haven't been back to Pahrump in what, seven or eight months. That old goat, Charley Ross, has been taking care of the property and he knows not to say anything to anybody. Hell, he might even shoot the bitch if she goes to the ranch."

"Did the Sheriff have any information on us?"

"I don't know Brian. Christina told her mom what she had heard and Elsie called me while I was in the Denver Hospital lobby, waiting for you to pick me up."

"What will we do in Reno? How will we survive?

"Just leave that to me. I am going to make arrangements to sell off the Pahrump property privately in a cash deal with my sister and her husband. That should take care of us financially for quite some time."

"Sure, until they track us down and lock us up for kidnapping the little angels."

"First of all, are you second-guessing me?

He looked at her and said, "Of course not Miss Paxton."

"Because Brian, if you are, you can leave any time."

"Sophie."

"That's Miss Paxton."

"Horseshit Sophie. I have stuck by you through all your decisions, good, bad or bullshit. I've been there with you, so don't push me anymore or you will be driving your ass around all by yourself. I'm just so tired of your disrespect. I'm telling you, don't talk to me like that anymore, because I'll let these kids go and I'll disappear."

"If I thought you meant that Brian, we would part company right here."

"Now it's your turn Sophie. Just shut up, sit back and enjoy the ride, because I don't want to hear anymore from you until we reach Delta."

"Brian."

"You heard me Sophie. Don't push me anymore."

"Brian. You're making a big mistake."

"Sometimes I think my big mistake was getting involved with you years ago; now I just tolerate your abusive behavior of me and anyone you come in contact with."

As their ride continued in silence, Sophie Paxton was boiling inside and felt herself conjuring up some way to resume her control over her companion.

42

At 9:45 am, Rosie, Juanita, and Tony walked into the Nye County Registrar's Office and requested to see any documentation concerning property ownership in the name of Sophie Paxton. They decided to check on ownership in all of her previous names also.

The clerk, whose name tag read Brandon Peck, Senior Clerk, wore a suit and vest. He looked about fifty-five, clean-shaven, 5'6", no more than 125lbs and wearing a visor. With his shiny bald head reflecting the light from the florescent fixtures above, he said, "Excuse me, no way."

Being met with what appeared to be complete resistance, Rosie was then told that the information she was requesting was not available to her without a court order and he was not prepared to help her without one.

Her response was, "Bullshit you bald headed bastard. That information is by law available on request to anyone seeking it, it's a matter of public record."

The man crossed his arms in front of his chest and said, "And you know that for a fact ma'am, or are you just using your vulgar language and what you think are big impressive words to try and intimidate me?"

"Sir, I tried to ask you nicely and you refused and then you tried to feed me some bull. So I'm asking you again, please provide me with the information I requested or I will report you to your supervisors and file a complaint against this office."

The clerk, not particularly happy with having been called a bald headed bastard, told Rosie, "Ma'am, if you don't agree with the way I run this office, you can go visit Judge Warren in the County Court House and file your complaint with him."

Trying to repair the damage created by the over zealous and excited woman, Tony asked the clerk if he could talk with him in private.

The clerk said, "I have nothing to say to you either."

Pulling out his ID and badge, Tony said, "You need to talk with me now or yes, we will go and see the judge before I lock your ass up for violating this woman's rights."

"I didn't violate her rights; she used abusive language and I don't have to tolerate that from anyone."

"And I suppose you have a witness to her abusive behavior?"

The clerk put his hands on his hips, looked straight at Tony and said, "You heard it all Agent Servantes."

"What I heard sir, was you refusing to cooperate with this woman's request."

"You know you heard more than that."

"Do you think your word will be taken over an agent of the FBI?"

"That's blackmail."

"You might call it that, but it can all be avoided."

"And how might that be- ah-Agent Servantes?"

"By giving this woman the information she needs to help her locate her granddaughter, who has been kidnapped."

Staring at Tony and then at Rosie, the clerk then turned around and walked to his desk and sat down in front of his computer and asked, "So what are the names you're checking on?"

Before the clerk even typed one name on the computer, Rosie said, "Thank you."

Reaching over to Tony, Rosie held his hand and said, "Thank you Hon."

Juanita sat in a chair by the door just watching all that went on and smiled when her mom looked at her.

Sophie Paxton was the legal owner of a twenty-acre plot of undeveloped land approximately ten miles out of town.

The deed to another piece of property was cross referenced to the name of Harvey and Sophie Stark, which was a twenty-five acre ranch about five miles out of town.

No other property was listed with the county belonging to any of the other names supplied by Rosie.

Looking up from his computer screen the clerk asked, "Is there anything else I can do for you?"

"Thank you again, I'm sorry I was so coarse with you. Yes I could use directions on how to get to the two properties you mentioned."

"I can print you out a map with directions; hold on."

Within a few minutes, Rosie had two maps and directions and was walking out the door.

The clerk turned facing the door and once again put his hands on his hips and said, "Good bye; and good riddance."

Juanita and Tony, not saying a word to the obnoxious man, just watched Rosie walk away, but knew she couldn't go anywhere without them because Juanita had the keys to the motor home.

Walking out slowly, Tony asked, "Rosie, didn't you forget something?"

"Forget something? Like what?"

"How about us, you twit."

With everyone loading into the motor home, Rosie decided she would drive, and Tony gave her directions as he looked at the map.

Twenty minutes later the motor home was turning off onto Wagon Wheel Road and Tony said, "This place is deserted; let's head for the other place."

Agreeing, Rosie turned the vehicle around and headed in the opposite direction and since it was on the other side of town, it took almost an hour to get to the unpaved road turn off called Old Mine Road.

A half-mile up the road they came to another turn-off with a small hand painted sign that said "Paxton Ranch."

Following the winding road, a large two-story farmhouse with a surrounding covered porch came into view. They proceeded at a slower pace and pulled up in front of the building.

Sitting on the porch in an old wooden swing, with a shotgun at his side, was Charley Ross, the caretaker of Paxton Ranch. The old man stared at the occupants of the vehicle through a pair of dust covered spectacles and he did not look happy to see the unexpected visitors.

As Rosie exited the motor home, old Charley said, "You can just get back in your vehicle little lady, turn around and get the hell out of here."

Instead, Rosie asked, "Sir, we're looking for Miss Paxton; can you help us?"

"I told you lady, turn around and get out of here, Miss Paxton ain't here and she's not coming back."

Tony opened the side door of the motor home and stepped out, then started walking toward the porch.

Picking up his shotgun, the old man said, "That goes for you too mister; I told you to get out of here. Unless you want a backside full of buckshot, you better listen to what I'm telling you both."

Taking a couple of steps backward, Tony told the old man, "Sir, I am an agent with the FBI and if you hold off shooting me for a few seconds, I'll show you my ID."

"Mister, I don't care what you want to show me, you're on private property, and I told you to leave."

"Sir, we are trying to get information about Sophie Paxton. She is involved in a kidnapping."

"She ain't been kidnapped, I talked to her yesterday, and she's fine, now get out of here."

"Sir, I didn't mean that she was kidnapped. She is involved in a kidnapping."

"Mister, I told you to get off this property."

"Sir, we need to talk with her."

Pointing the shotgun at the sky, the old buzzard squeezed the trigger and a very loud blast caught everyone's attention.

Tony hit the ground grabbing his service revolver while Rosie ducked down in her seat. Juanita let out a scream and Sandy started barking.

Tony rolled over and got cover from the front fenders of the motor home.

The old man said, "I told you I would shoot; now get out of here."

"Are you crazy old man, threatening a government agent with a weapon, now put the shotgun down?"

"Sonny, I'm not putting nothing down; you people are trespassing and now you're leaving."

"If we leave like this, I promise you I'll be back with more law than you want to see. Now put the gun down so we can talk."

The old man stared at Tony for a few seconds, then walked over to the wall and leaned his shotgun against a chair by the door and said, "Ok, you can come up here, but I ain't telling you nothing about Miss Paxton. She's a good woman and I don't want to hurt her."

Returning his revolver to its holster, Tony slowly got back to his feet while Rosie stepped out of the vehicle. They then both walked to the porch.

Juanita remained in the motor home but asked if it was okay to let Sandy out to stretch her legs and maybe relieve her self.

Rosie said softly, "its okay dear; you can let her out but bring her out on a leash."

Sitting back down on the porch swing, old Charley watched cautiously as Tony and Rosie stepped up on the porch and sat down in the two chairs against the wall.

Pointing at the shotgun, Rosie asked, "Sir would you mind if I laid the gun down on the porch? It might fall over and go off again."

"It can't do that ma'am, it ain't got no more shells in it; only had the one." But if it makes you nervous, I'll move it."

Rosie said, "Thank you sir."

Then she asked, "What is your name sir?"

"Ma'am, my name is Charley Ross. And you are?"

Tony spoke up and introduced himself and then started to introduce Rosie when she cut him off saying, "Excuse me, Charley was speaking to me. You'll get your turn, just hold your horses. Charley, my name is Rosie Castro."

The old man liked that. So much that he started laughing out loud and told Tony, "She got you there sonny; she got spunk."

Rosie started again, "Charley, my granddaughter was kidnapped in New York over two months ago and we know that Miss Paxton and her companion Brian Doyle, not only have my granddaughter, but another little girl also."

"I think you're wrong missy. Miss Paxton wouldn't do something like that. But that Brian, now he's a bad man."

"Charley, I'm an ex-police officer. During the commission of a crime in New Jersey, Miss Paxton's son, Lester was shot and killed."

"You shot Lester?"

"Actually Charley, my partner at the time shot and killed Lester, after he shot me twice."

"Lester shot you?"

"Yes he did. He tried to kill me and he almost succeeded. I was injured bad enough that I had to retire from the police force."

"What kind of crime did he do?"

'He was involved in drugs Charley."

Charley said, "That boy was always trouble."

"Miss Paxton blames me for her son's death and she took my granddaughter to get back at me."

"Ma'am, I've known Miss Paxton for over forty years, back before she married that shoe salesman Sam Taylor, then Lester's dad, Jimmy

233

Stark. I never knew Mr. Paxton. He died before we had a chance to meet."

"Charley, we really need to find Miss Paxton. Would you please help us? Would you please help me get my granddaughter back?

"Ma'am, I don't know where she's at."

"Where did she call you from?"

"I don't know that either; she didn't tell me. She just told me to keep an eye on the ranch until she sells it to the Larsen's and that she would take care of me later."

"Who are the Larsens, and do you think they know where she might be staying?"

"They're kin to Miss Paxton."

"Kin, Charley?"

"Mrs. Larsen is Miss Paxton's sister."

"Do you think she knows where her sister Sophie is?"

"I don't know; you have to ask her."

Rosie looked at Tony who had his arms folded on his chest and asked, "Tony, do you have anything you want to ask Charley?"

"Mr. Ross, how long has it been since you talked to Miss Paxton?"

"I told you before sonny. I talked to her yesterday."

"And you don't know where she called you from?"

"Ain't you been listening sonny?"

"It's Agent Servantes, or Tony; not Sonny. Okay Charley?"

Charley laughed a little and said, "A little touchy, huh Agent Servantes?"

"Charley, please answer my questions."

"Agent, I don't know where she is, how to get a hold of her, or when she is coming back. Does that about cover all your questions?"

Tony just shook his head and said, "Okay Rosie, it's your call. What's next?"

"We're going to talk with the Larsens. How do we get there, Charley?"

Using a small stick, Charley drew a crude map on the porch floor and said, "That should get you there, but I still think you're wrong about Miss Paxton."

43

Leaving the Paxton Ranch and Charley Ross in their rear view mirrors, they drove slowly down the bumpy dirt road. Tony, who was now driving the motor home, turned onto Old Mine Road.

Up ahead they could see a van on the side of the road with its hood up and a woman standing next to it waving her arms for the motor home to stop.

Pulling up next to the van, Tony asked, "Can we be of some assistance?"

The woman walked over to Tony's side of the van and said, "Yes you can Agent Servantes, you are interfering with a Bureau investigation."

"And who are you?"

"My name is Agent Marsha Beloff and at the moment I am assigned to the temporary field office set up right here in Pahrump."

"You mind showing me some identification Agent Beloff?"

Just then, Tony heard, "She doesn't have to Servantes, but do you want to see mine again?"

"Well, Russ Taylor. You're an awful long way from Toledo, aren't you?"

"What the hell are you doing here Servantes?"

Rosie couldn't stay out of this conversation any longer. "He's on vacation Agent Taylor, and he's here with me looking for my granddaughter. Do you have a problem with that?"

"Miss Castro, is it?"

Rosie said, "You know damn well what my name is."

"This is none of your business Miss Castro, so please stay out of it and be quiet."

"BE QUIET? You asshole. You don't tell me to be quiet. I'll shove your ID up your ass along with your balls and then we'll see how quiet you can be."

"I'm sorry Miss Castro, that didn't come out right. I apologize. But it is an FBI investigation."

"Investigation? You guys haven't done shit. I've given the FBI more info than they've given me."

"I'm very sorry if you're unhappy with the way the investigation is going Miss Castro, but we won't rest until we locate the missing children."

"Yeah I bet."

"Agent Servantes, may I speak with you in private?"

Tony pulled the motor home over to the side of the road and started to get out when Rosie said, "Tony, don't take any shit from him."

Walking down the road with Tony about 100 feet before he spoke, Agent Taylor finally stopped and asked, "Tony, what the hell are you doing here?"

"What am I doing here? What the hell are you doing here?"

Agent Taylor said, "This is a bureau investigation, and I have been assigned to watch for the kidnappers."

"What, they called you in all the way from Ohio just for this investigation? Bullshit! What's the real reason you're here?"

"Servantes, I don't have to answer to you, this is a bureau investigation and that's all you need to know."

Tony said, "I've had just about enough of your bullshit Russ, we're out of here."

The two men walked back to the vehicles in silence.

Looking at the woman now standing next to Agent Taylor, Tony asked, "And I suppose you're an agent from Ohio also?"

Very quickly Agent Taylor responded, "You don't have to answer that. It's none of his business."

That told Tony right away that she was not an agent or any other law enforcement officer and something didn't smell right about this whole situation.

From past experience, Tony knew that most officials with any branch of enforcement would have to identify themselves once questioned.

Trying to provoke either one of them, Tony asked, "So I guess you're just a hooker he picked up on your way to work?"

All it brought was a dirty look from Agent Taylor and a response of, "We're done here and so are you Servantes. Take your Puerto Rican bitch and get the hell out of here."

Before Tony had a chance to answer the asshole, Rosie was screaming, "What did you call me you mother fucker?"

Tony had enough common sense to get out of Rosie's way as she came charging out of the motor home.

She hit Agent Taylor with a tackle that would make any football coach proud. He grunted as he got hit and fell backwards onto a prickly cactus.

As Agent Taylor lay there in agony for a few seconds, Tony said, "I guess you hurt the lady's feelings, Taylor?"

"Screw you and her too Servantes."

Trying to get back on his feet, the agent spread his legs just enough for Rosie to plant her size 8 sneaker right in his groin, then she said, "Now we're done here."

The woman tried to help Agent Taylor up, but being the kind of person he was, he just said, "Get the hell away from me, I don't need any help."

Laughing as they drove away, Tony and Rosie found it very hard to explain what had just happened to Juanita, who had woken up from Sandy's barking.

Tony looked at Juanita and said through his laughter, "Your Mom just tackled the opposition and then kicked a field goal."

Of course Juanita had no idea what Tony was talking about. With her mom and Tony laughing so much, she just said, "The sleeping pill I took before is starting to kick in, so I'm going back to bed while you two enjoy whatever has you cracking up so much."

Tony took out his cell phone and called his office back in New York to talk with his supervisor. Al Wallace was out so he left a message for him to please call back.

About five minutes after they turned onto the paved highway heading back to downtown Pahrump, Rosie's cell phone started playing the new tune that had been programmed on to it, "I can see clearly now the rain has gone."

On the screen it read, "Unidentified Caller."

Answering, Rosie said calmly, "Yes, this is Rosie."

"Well hello Detective Castro. Enjoying the desert scenery around beautiful Pahrump?"

"Hello asshole. Or should I say Mr. Doyle, Mr. Brian Doyle?"

"That would be nice detective."

Rosie said, "I want to talk to my granddaughter Mr. Doyle."

"That's not going to happen, detective."

"Where are you, you bastard?"

"Are you and Agent Servantes enjoying your trip to Nevada?"

Rosie looked at Tony and asked him to please pull over to the side.

Rosie asked Doyle, "Why are you doing this? When you're caught, they'll put you and that crazy woman away for life. Is that anyway to spend your few remaining years of life?"

"That's why we decided to disappear for good, with no more contact. So enjoy your visit to that hot, dry paradise and we'll enjoy our new choice of environment."

Tony held up a note that read, "Keep him on as long as you can." Tony was on the line with the field office in Las Vegas trying to get a trace on him.

"Oh, by the way Brian, how is your son doing? Is he still in custody?"

Mr. Doyle was suddenly quiet, but then Miss Paxton put in her two cents after grabbing the phone, "I suppose you have figured out by now Detective Castro who my son was. I know that you were responsible for his death and also that you will never see your granddaughter again."

"You can't hide forever Miss Paxton; you will be found and prosecuted. That I promise you."

Laughing very loudly, the wicked Sophie Paxton said, "Goodbye Detective Castro. I'll give your granddaughter a kiss tonight as I read her a story that her new grandma has picked out."

Rosie said, "If you had raised your son properly, he could have provided you with grandchildren of your own."

Sophie Paxton must have been fuming, but all she said was, "Goodbye Detective. She'll never hear of you again."

As the phone went silent, Rosie looked at Tony and asked, "Well?"

"They are somewhere in Utah, that's all I got."

Rosie thought for a few seconds and then said, "I stayed on the phone for over four minutes with them. Wouldn't you think they knew we were trying to track them down and use their call to zero in on them?"

Tony said, "Who knows what's going on in their sick minds."

Tony started the motor home engine, put the shift lever in drive, and started to pull back onto the highway when suddenly a tire blew out.

Pulling back onto the shoulder so he could check out which tire it was, there came a second explosion and the vehicle leaned quickly to the left.

Getting out and checking the tires, Tony saw that both left rear tires were blown out and as Rosie came around the rear of the vehicle he grabbed her and they both fell to the ground.

Asking him, "What the hell are you doing Tony?" He pointed to the side of the motor home at the bullet holes just below the window.

Rosie screamed, got up quickly, and ran to the side door calling out, "Juanita, Juanita. Are you okay?"

Lying in a small pool of blood, Juanita had been struck by one of the bullets in her upper back and was moaning, "Mom, Mom, help me," then she passed out.

Rosie yelled out, "Tony, Juanita's been shot! She needs a paramedic! Come quick Tony."

One more shot hit the side window, blowing the glass all over the bed.

Tony was on his phone quickly calling 911. The paramedics were dispatched out of Pahrump along with the Sheriff and his deputy.

With his service revolver in his hand, Tony went back outside and carefully looked around the rear of the vehicle in the direction of the shooter.

Checking Juanita's wound, Rosie could see that there was an entrance wound and an exit wound, so she held a towel over both and applied pressure until the paramedics arrived.

44

Hiller Mountain was given its name in 1840 by the townspeople of Delta, named after Ezekiel Thurston Hiller. The early explorer was the first man to stake out his claim to the one-time worthless rocky hillside.

Following directions supplied by Miss Paxton, Brian Doyle pulled off the highway onto a winding narrow paved road that was posted, "Road ends one mile ahead." Following the road to the end, Doyle was directed to turn left onto a dirt road where he could see a cabin in the distance at the far end of the property they had entered.

Parking the Suburban in front of the steps leading up to the rustic looking cabin, Doyle, Miss Paxton and the two girls walked up the fifteen steps, all the time checking out the view as they went higher and higher.

The cabin looked liked something out of the "Beverly Hillbillies". All the wood of the cabin looked dried out and had a gray appearance. The tall trees surrounding the area all appeared in fine healthy condition but the shrubs and other plants all looked dead or dying from lack of water.

Entering the building, Brian Doyle, was surprised to see that everything seemed so well kept inside considering its outside appearance.

Miss Paxton, not wanting to waste much time, escorted the girls to their room and told them to get ready for bed.

Lisa spoke up and said, "But Miss Paxton, it's not even dark yet."

With harshness in her voice, the old woman told her, "You just do what I told you. I don't want any back talk from you or I'll smack your bottom."

Leaving the room, Sophie Paxton then told Brian, "Let's go sit out on the porch for a while. We need to talk without any little ears around us."

After sitting on the front porch of the cabin for a short while, Sophie Paxton and Brian Doyle started reflecting on the past couple of months and all that had happened since they left New York.

Brian asked, "Sophie, you haven't told me who owns this wonderful old cabin?"

Miss Paxton said, "This cabin belongs to an old friend of the Cotter family. It was partially owned by my grandfather and his hunting buddies."

"There's no problem using it?" Brian asked.

The old woman said, "None at all Brian." The three families have shared ownership and it has been going on for sixty-five years, with the cabin remaining vacant at least 90% of the time. It occasionally gets used by some of the hunters in the other families during the winter months, but not very often."

Sitting and just reflecting, the conversation went silent.

Brian was to later find out that there were no utilities supplied by the county. No phone service, no electric, gas or running water. When he asked about the utilities, she told him. "Water comes from a well that is fed by underground mountain springs and is very clean and crystal clear. The lighting and electrical needs are taken care of by a commercial diesel generator that's located in a barn fifty feet to the rear of the cabin."

Brian asked, "What about heating and cooking?"

She said, "The two large efficient fireplaces and an extra large propane supply tank provide the heating and cooking needs. It's very efficient Brian."

Miss Paxton went back inside to check on the children and start a small fire in the fireplace to take the chill out of the bedroom.

The two little girls had tucked themselves into bed and with the fire in the fireplace warming up the room, they were soon fast asleep.

Miss Paxton rejoined Brian on the porch to continue their conversation.

After talking with him a little more, Miss Paxton informed him of her decision to live in the cabin for several months before they would move on to another location. They would have limited contact with the outside world except for food or other supplies they might find necessary.

The plan was still to finally end up in the Reno area but that wouldn't be until Miss Paxton sold her property in Pahrump to her sister and brother-in-law.

With a smile on his face, Brian Doyle, looked out at the beautiful view of the valley and surrounding property and said, "I can get used to this kind of living Sophie."

45

The paramedics out of Pahrump had shown up at the motor home approximately ten minutes after the 911 dispatcher received the call. With great care and expertise, they stabilized Juanita finding that her wound was not life threatening although she had lost a lot of blood.

The bullet had entered Juanita's right shoulder, passed through the muscle and exited above her right breast, not hitting any major arteries, then ending up in the mattress.

The sleeping pills that Juanita had taken earlier helped slow down her respiration and blood pressure, which in turn helped slow down some of the bleeding.

While Juanita was being transferred to the local hospital with Rosie accompanying her in the ambulance, Tony was giving the sheriff a statement.

A tow truck had been called to the scene to haul the motor home back into town after it was examined and the path of the bullet from the shooter was determined.

As the sheriff and his deputies searched the area, Tony called the FBI field office to inform them of the situation. He reported the actions of Agent Taylor and a suspicious female companion.

After some inquiries made by the bureau field agent, Tony was informed that Agent Russel Taylor was not working in any official capacity. He was in fact on an unapproved leave of absence with reprimands pending. Also, the woman accompanying him was not an agent with the FBI.

Tony asked if there was any additional information on the kidnappers. He was told that there was nothing new to report but the investigation was still underway and getting more intensive.

Tony was told that the last contact and sighting of any kind was documented at a hospital in Denver. Miss Paxton visited the hospital there for a prosthetic leg repair and was instructed to remain for an examination but she declined.

There was also a possible ID in Grand Junction, Colorado. But that ID was still pending verification. After that they seemed to disappear from sight.

The agent in charge asked Tony for the location of the shooting. He also told him he would meet him at the hospital as soon as he called in some recruits. He told Tony, "Nobody shoots at an agent of the government and gets away with it."

Once Tony thanked the agent and got off the phone, he called Rosie to find out Juanita's condition. The good news was that Juanita would only require a short hospital stay, maybe two or three days. The bad news was that one of the bullets ruptured the motor home's fuel tank.

The sheriff had no leads on the shooter but said he would not rest until he located the individual responsible for this awful crime.

Making sure that Juanita was comfortable and safe, Tony and Rosie registered at one of the local motels. The motor home was taken to a repair shop after it was released by the sheriff's department, which authorized the okay to do the repairs.

Three days had passed with Rosie spending many hours with Juanita at the hospital, and the rest of the time she and Tony questioned local business owners about Miss Paxton and Brian Doyle.

Most of the people they had talked with didn't know either of the kidnappers. The few people who were familiar with the pair told them that they kept to themselves most of the time. They were a strange couple who didn't welcome visitors at their ranch when they were around.

Driving a car that they had rented in town, Rosie and Tony visited the Paxton Ranch daily to talk with Charley to ask if there had been any communication with Miss Paxton, but the answer was always no.

Talking with the Larsens was futile, as they did not want to co-operate at all. Even with a visit from the FBI, they refused to admit that they had any communication with Paxton or Doyle.

Helen Larsen refused to talk with Rosie at all, except calling her the bitch that killed her nephew.

Henry Larsen was verbal, telling Tony and Rosie, "Take your asses back to New York and leave the good people of Pahrump to live their lives in peace."

He was also very threatening, telling Rosie, "You better leave here while you can still walk, lady."

Rosie asked him, "Are you threatening me, Mr. Larsen?"

His answer was, "Accidents happen!"

Leaving the Larsen home, Tony and Rosie realized that all they could do was sit and wait for something to happen.

It was obvious to both of them that the sick minds went hand and hand with the kidnappers. As Rosie put it, "Those kin folks are a little sick upstairs."

Tony said, "Seems to run in their family genes."

46

After two weeks of questioning the locals, checking out phony leads and constant arguing with Tony, Rosie was getting frustrated. The constant bickering was pushing her and Tony further apart. She would say, "It's just the way things are going. I just don't know what to do next."

Rosie and Juanita were back living in the motor home after the fuel tank repair. Tony was still staying at the motel trying to give the women a little more space. Rosie had made arrangements with the local hardware store owner to park the motor home in the rear of his very large parking lot.

Because agents from Las Vegas FBI had entered the picture and were questioning the Larsens on a regular basis, they had retained an attorney to get an injunction to stop the harassment.

Tony had been in contact with his supervisor back in New York and the pressure was being put on him to return to his job. He was asked to start putting pressure on Rosie to give up her crazy idea of finding the kidnappers and stop interfering with an FBI investigation.

Knowing it was time to return to New York because the solid leads had run out and their hunt for the kidnappers had stalled out, Tony tried to choose his words carefully when he talked to Rosie.

During the past week he had tried pointing out the fact that nothing more was coming out of their investigation and maybe it would be a good idea to turn everything over to the bureau. But Rosie deeply resented Tony's suggestion.

The idea of going back to New York without her granddaughter Lisa was unacceptable. She told her dear friend, "If you feel that you have to go, then go. I am staying, even if it means I have to get a job here and become a local myself. Those bastards have a history here and I know they will show up sometime. I will be here when that time comes."

The Sheriff and the FBI who had worked diligently to find the gunman who shot out the tires on the motor home and came very close to ending the life of Rosie's daughter were at a complete stand still.

Charley Ross had been picked up and questioned about the shooting but it proved to be unwarranted.

The Larsens were questioned extensively a second time, but both had ironclad alibis for the time the shooting took place. They chose once again to contact their attorney, just in case there were any further repercussions and inform him of the FBI violation of the injunction.

Juanita, although very strong in her heart, believed in her mom's convictions but talked with her that night. As the tears rolled down her cheeks, she said, "Mom, I love you very much and I could never love or miss Lisa anymore than I do at this moment, but I can't do this anymore. I'm not as strong as you. Please, let's go home. Let the FBI find Lisa. Please, I want to go back to New York."

Hugging her daughter and gently wiping the tears from her cheeks, Rosie told her, "Sweetheart, I can't leave now. To me it would be giving up on everything we've been through. That would make me feel that those sons of bitches won and I couldn't live with that."

"Mom, please?"

"Juanita Honey, Tony is going back home tomorrow. Fly back with him. I'll be fine by myself and I promise I'll stay in touch with you. I'll keep Sandy with me and we'll try to fit in around here."

Tony was standing only a few feet away and heard everything Rosie said, and as she held out her hand to welcome him to come closer, the three hugged in a very warm and strong embrace.

Rosie asked Tony, "Please Hon, watch out for Juanita and keep me informed as to any new information on those bastards."

"Rosie, isn't there anything I can do to change your mind about staying?"

"Tony, you've tried that before and you could try all night. But nothing is going to change my mind. I'm staying! That's it! Get used to it!"

"Okay, I'm going to work on transportation for Juanita and me so you two can spend some quality time together tonight. I'll see you both in the morning."

Deciding to take a walk around town, Rosie and Juanita stopped at the local ice cream store, got a couple of cones, sat for a few minutes watching the light amount of traffic drive by and then continued on the walk.

Although most of the stores were closed for the night, the ones that were still open had only a few customers, who in most cases seemed to be only browsing and killing time on the unusually warm night for the time of year.

Walking past a row of newly constructed stores that were set back off the street, Rosie pointed out that all three were in different phases of completion with "Help Wanted" signs in the windows of two of them.

The store on the far left was a hair and nail salon set to open in one month. The middle store was called, "The Yarn Barn," and would also be ready for a grand opening in one month. The store on the far right was set to open in one week and it was called, "The Egg Stop." There were two positions available for employees, one for a dishwasher and the other for a waitress.

Stopping in front of the open door and looking in, a man who was doing a little bit of finish work on painting around the counter asked, "Can I help you ladies?"

Rosie jokingly asked, "So what's the boss like?"

The man answered, "He's pretty decent. He comes from back east somewhere, I think maybe New York. But you know those New Yorkers, most of them have some pretty bad attitudes and he could have a rough time out here."

Rosie, speaking in the most exaggerated east coast New York accent she possibly could, said,

"Hey, yo, I'm from New Yawk and I tink I'll do good here. Ya know what I mean?"

The man laughed for a few seconds and then asked, "What kind of job are you looking for?"

"Right now any job would be good, but I prefer a job as a waitress, I think it's something I can handle."

"Do you have any experience as a waitress?"

"Looks like a lot more than you have at painting."

The man turned around to see what Rosie was talking about, when he noticed paint dripping down off the counter onto the freshly varnished floor and said, "Shit."

"So where can I find the boss?" Rosie asked.

"You can meet him here tomorrow morning. Right now I need to get back to doing my job so I don't get fired. Goodnight ladies."

Rosie smiled and said, "It doesn't look like you're ready to serve eggs yet."

"We will be soon. Like I said, I got to go back to work. Have a nice night."

259

47

While the sun was setting over the treetops in the western sky, Brian Doyle and Sophie Paxton watched from the front porch of the cabin at the base of Hiller Mountain.

Lisa Soto and Elizabeth Schorr sat playing cards on a large round rug on the cabin floor. Talking softly to one another, Lisa asked, "Do you think we will ever see our Mommies again?"

Elizabeth only shrugged her shoulders, looked at the front door of the cabin and then said, "Maybe we could run away and find somebody to take us home."

Lisa whispered softly, "I bet my mommy is worried about me and is crying every night."

Starting to cry herself, Elizabeth said, "I miss my mommy and daddy so much and I hope they find me."

Both girls were now crying as they lay down on the rug and soon fell off to sleep.

Remarking about how beautiful the sunsets were and how peaceful the surroundings were in that part of the country, Brian said, "Sophie, I could spend the rest of my life here and never go to a city again."

"You old fool. I give you a couple of months. After that, I bet you'll be happy to visit the city, if just to talk to someone else besides me."

"Sophie, I've been trapped in a car and crappy motel rooms with you and those two little brats for over three months, and I still say, this is paradise."

"Okay Mister Paradise, how about chopping some wood for the fireplace, while I go down to the general store for some groceries."

Brian smiled and said, "You got it Mama Sophie."

She was really not amused, but she said, "Very funny Brian. Keep an eye on the kids. They're awfully quiet in there."

Brian told her, "Pick me up a box of Mounds bars please. If they don't have any, make sure they order a couple of boxes and I'll pick them up when they come in."

"You and those damn candy bars. Don't you know by now that those things will rot your teeth?"

"If you had paid attention all these years we've been together, you would have noticed that I don't eat any other candy and my teeth are in great condition for a sixty-two year old man."

"What the hell is the difference? It's all sugar and those teeth of yours won't last for ever without some dental care."

"The difference is the flavor and the texture. It's like nothing else out there."

"Yeah sure, I'm sold. Eat them till you drop you old fool."

48

The drive into McCarran International Airport in Las Vegas to drop off Juanita and Tony was a very tearful and somber trip. Tony kept trying ever so hard to talk Rosie into selling the motor home and returning to New York herself.

Trying to make it clear that she would not return without her granddaughter, Rosie said, "Enough already, Tony. You're not changing my mind. Either accept it or change the subject. I'm not going back home yet."

The drive to the airport took approximately forty-five minutes and because of the motor home's size, it was determined that Rosie would just drop them off at the loading and unloading zone. With quick hugs, kisses, and a tearful goodbye, Rosie told Juanita. "Call me as soon as you touch down in New York so I don't worry."

Driving back to Pahrump by herself, with Sandy sleeping in the rear bedroom, Rosie pulled over on the side of the road at a turn off, put the motor home in park and cried like a baby for a few minutes. It was the first time since all of this started that she was completely alone. The emotions in her had reached a boiling point and she knew she couldn't hold it back any longer.

With no one to see or hear her, she just let it out. Emotions that had been bottled up inside her for over three months emptied out like water flowing over a dam. After that, Rosie dried her tears, took a few heavy breaths and continued on her trip back to Pahrump.

The next morning Rosie had an appointment with her, hopefully, new boss, at "The Egg Stop." She was sitting on a folding chair outside the front door with Sandy lying by her side, when he pulled up and parked in front.

Getting out of his old Ford LTD station wagon, the man walked up to Rosie and extended his hand.

Sandy got up and started barking until Rosie told her to stop and lie back down.

"We haven't been properly introduced," he said. I'm Michael Refino, originally from Brooklyn, now the proud owner of this new money making establishment."

Rosie smiled and said, "You clean up pretty nice Michael. You look a lot better without all that paint all over your face and clothes."

"And you are, might I ask?"

"I'm sorry Michael. I'm Rosie, Rosie Castro, originally from Jersey, by way of a few years in Brooklyn."

"Well Miss Castro, you still looking for a job in the exciting profitable food service industry?"

Laughing as she asked, "You do drugs, Mike? This is Pahrump, not exactly Vegas. But yes, I'm ready."

"No drugs ma'am, not since the big drug bust at the Rolling Stones concert many years ago, but I do have a few drinks now and then. Will that do, Miss Castro?"

"That works fine for me, but if you don't start calling me Rosie, we're going to have a problem."

After talking about and agreeing on working hours, salary and Mike making friends with Sandy, Rosie and her new boss went inside "The Egg Stop" and checked out possible changes for the opening in a few days.

After unpacking boxes of new dishes, cups, and glasses and more pots and pans than Rosie thought she would ever see in one place, Michael suggested they take a break and go have lunch at one of the local competitors down the street.

"You mean my first day on the job; the boss is taking me to lunch?"

"Don't get too used to it. I heard the boss is really a cheap bastard."

Rosie smiled and said, "Lunch is on me boss. From the looks of things, you're going to need all your money just to make it through the first week."

Tossing her a set of keys to the store, Michael said, "Very funny. Lock the door and I'll meet you out at the car Rosie."

Driving to the other end of town, the LTD wagon pulled up in front of a trailer that was now called, "The Weenie Wagon," and Rosie looked at Michael and said, "Nice choice, Mister Big Spender."

"Best hot dogs in town Rosie. You'll thank me later."

"They have to go a lot to beat Nathans."

"We'll get a couple with everything on them and you be the judge."

After a very enjoyable treat of hot dogs and beer, Rosie and Michael returned to "The Egg Stop" to continue getting things in order for the grand opening in a few days.

From all that happened that first day, it looked like Rosie was in good hands, for a while anyway. But things always seem to change as time goes by.

Sitting in the folding chair in front of "The Egg Stop" when Rosie and Michael arrived was FBI Agent Russel Taylor.

When Rosie saw him she told Michael, "That's that asshole agent who gave me all kinds of trouble a couple weeks ago. I think he had something to do with my daughter getting shot."

"Do you need to talk to him?"

"I don't want to, but I guess I should."

"I'll get rid of him if you want?"

"No, but thank you Michael, I'm sure I can handle him."

Getting out of the car slowly and walking up to the obnoxious agent, Rosie asked, "And what is it you want now, Taylor?"

"Miss Castro, I don't want to get off on the wrong foot."

"It's too late Taylor, you're an asshole, and I already know that. Now what do you want?"

"I want to clear the air."

"Then leave town. You're stinking it up."

"Please Miss Castro, no more wise cracks. We need to talk."

"Why?" Rosie asked.

"Is there somewhere we can talk in private?"

Michael asked, "Do you two need to be alone?"

Answering quickly, Rosie said, "No Michael. Whatever he has to say to me, I want a witness, because if he gives me too much shit, I may be tempted to kill the bastard."

Michael smiled and said, "Come inside and we can sit down away from prying eyes."

Across the road at the convenience store, there were already a half dozen people watching the man who drove up in the government car.

After Rosie unlocked the door, they all went inside and sat down at one of the tables.

The agent made a remark about the smell of the fresh paint and how strong it was. Rosie couldn't resist one more zing, "It smelled pretty good in here before you walked in Taylor."

As Michael smiled, the agent said, "I'll just ignore that shot Miss Castro."

"What do you want Taylor? We have work to do."

Getting up from his chair and pacing back and forth, Agent Taylor decided to open up and talk to Rosie freely.

"Miss Castro, I don't know how much you and Agent Servantes found out before his return to New York. But I assure you. I had nothing to do with your daughter getting shot and the attack on you and Servantes."

"Well that's awfully nice to know that the FBI didn't assign a killer to take us out. But what the hell are you doing out here anyway? You're based in Ohio?"

"I took a leave of absence from the bureau for personal reasons."

Rosie asked, "And?"

"Sophie Paxton was once married to my father, a fact that I don't care to admit. But, nonetheless it's true and I'm not proud of it."

"Wait a minute, she's your stepmother?"

"Please, not that close. She tried at one point to recruit me to assist her at throwing you off her trail. When I refused and told her to turn her self in, she screamed at me and hung up."

Standing up, Rosie asked, "Do you have any idea where they might be?"

"Last sighting and contact was in Utah. Just so you know. There have been twenty more agents assigned to the investigation now."

"What about the shooting, do you have any idea who is behind it?"

"No I don't."

"Well someone out there knows."

Agent Taylor said, "I've been in touch with the Sheriff and he feels it was just a random act. But he's still investigating."

"Well what do we do now?" Rosie asked.

"The agent sat back down and said, "I talked with my supervisor and explained my connection with the kidnappers. He ordered me back to Ohio. But before my return, I wanted to tell you where I stood and that I have no other connection with those people."

"Well I have to admit Russel, I was wrong about you. But you better get in touch with Tony Servantes and fill him in. He still thinks you're a piece of shit."

"That's it for me Miss Castro. I've got a plane to catch in Vegas. I'm sorry for your troubles and I'm sorry for the way I acted towards you."

"Thank you Russel."

"I hope you locate your granddaughter soon."

With that the agent got up, shook hands with Rosie and Michael and then left.

Rosie looked at Michael and said, "I'll try not to let my personal problems get in the way of my work."

Taking Rosie's hand in his, Michael said, "Whatever I can do to help, please don't be afraid to ask."

"When we have time to sit and talk, Michael, I'll tell you everything that's happened, if you're interested?"

"From what I've heard so far, I can't wait, Rosie."

49

It was November 1st and an early morning snowstorm had caught most New Yorkers by surprise. One month had passed by since Juanita's return trip back home and on this cold and wet afternoon, she was heading home from the market when her cell phone started buzzing.

Rosie had made it a practice to call her daughter every other day and she had already talked to her that morning, so Juanita knew it was not her mother. The caller ID was not familiar so she just answered, "Hello."

"Mommy, it's me, Lisa."

Dropping her bag of groceries on the ground, Juanita said, "Lisa, honey, where are you?"

Now speaking a little softer, Lisa answered, "I'm in a cabin and Papa Brian is outside chopping wood."

"Where is the old woman honey?"

"Miss Paxton went for a ride somewhere. She left two days ago and hasn't come back yet."

"Be careful sweetheart. Don't let the man see or hear you on the phone."

"I can see him outside mommy. He's still chopping wood."

"Lisa honey, do you know what state you're in? Where is the cabin located?"

"I don't know mommy, nobody told me. I think we're in a place called Utah."

"Are you calling from a house phone?"

"No, it's a cell phone."

"Sweetheart, listen carefully. After you end the call, you need to clear my number off of the phone."

"But I want to come home mommy, I don't like it here."

"Lisa, please listen carefully. You're going to have to clear the last number called from the phone so the man doesn't know you called me. I'm going to explain how to do it then you're going to do what I tell you then end the call."

"But mommy, I don't...."

"Sweetheart, please listen to mommy. If you can, call me tomorrow. I will have someone here who can trace the call and find out where you are, then I will come and get you."

Starting to cry, Lisa said, "Mommy, please hurry and come get me."

"I will sweetheart. Now listen close."

Being wise enough to know that this call from her daughter should not go on much longer (although there were so many things she wanted to ask), she knew it had to end quickly for her daughter's safety.

Juanita explained to her daughter how to erase the last call made. After that, they both started to cry before she told her how much she loved her. Although it hurt to do it, she ended the call.

Immediately, Juanita called Tony Servantes. His first response was, "Put the cell phone away and be careful not to lose the number Lisa called from."

"Tony, I need to call mom."

"Don't use the cell. Call from another phone. I'll be there as soon as I get instructions on how to proceed from my supervisor."

"Tony, I'll be home in about ten minutes. I'm on my way home from the market now."

"Okay, I'll meet you there as soon as I can. Juanita, this is a good sign. We'll get her back."

"Bye Tony. I'll call Mom as soon as I get home and tell her what you said."

Trying to pick up her groceries that she had dropped, Juanita scrambled putting cans and vegetables in her jacket pockets and down her blouse. The bags had broken open and some things she just left on the pavement and started to run for home.

50

Over the past month, Rosie had become a very efficient waitress working at "The Egg Stop." She met many of the townspeople, most of whom paid her compliments and thanked her boss for the service they provided.

The breakfast eatery had become a popular morning stop and Michael, after only a few weeks since opening, had to hire extra help.

The 90-degree temperature in Pahrump, on that morning when Juanita called to tell her mom about Lisa, felt more like 110, as the sweat poured down from Rosie's brow.

Rosie got Michael's attention and let him know that she had to step outside to talk with her daughter. He could see that she was in a panic situation so he just said, "Go! Go! We can handle everything."

Juanita told her mom everything that Lisa had said, but Rosie kept asking questions that her daughter had no answers for and it was frustrating.

As Rosie paced back and forth on the porch in front of the three businesses, one of the women who worked in the hair and nail salon next door came out of the store and tried to get Rosie's attention.

In a very angry voice, Rosie asked, "Jill, what the hell do you want?"

Jill Stewart, who had only been working at "The Curl and Polished Nail" since it opened three days earlier, told Rosie, "Helen Larsen was in the salon first thing this morning and told the owner her sister Sophie was in town. She is staying at her house for a couple of days to finalize the sale of her property to her and her husband."

Letting it soak in, Rosie told Juanita, "I'll call you back dear. I was just told Sophie Paxton is here in town."

"Mom, don't hang up. What are you going to do?"

"Sweetheart, I'll call you back. Stay by the phone."

"Mom, wait." Juanita begged. But it was too late, the call was ended.

Walking back into the restaurant, Rosie quickly made her way over to Michael and told him, "Hon, I've got to take off the rest of the day. I just got word that Sophie Paxton, the woman who kidnapped my granddaughter, is just outside of town staying at her sister's home."

"Rosie, what are you going to do?" Michael asked.

"First I need to call the FBI and give them the information and the address. Then I'm going to my trailer and get my gun. Then I'm going to pay the Larsens a visit."

"Rosie, you better think this out a little more before you go off halfcocked and jumping into the fire."

"What do you suggest Michael? That I should just sit around here and wait for the fucking FBI? They can't seem to find their peckers in the men's room. No, this time I'm going to take control."

"Rosie, call the sheriff at least. Let him go with you. He's a good man and he'll help."

"Michael, while I make the call to… Oh shit! I forgot his name. I need to get my purse. Please call the Sheriff for me and I'll call the Vegas FBI office. I'll tell him not to waste time because I'm not going to wait very long for him."

As Rosie went to get her purse in the back room, Michael called Sheriff Norton Majors and explained all that Rosie had told him.

The Sheriff said, "Mike, you tell that crazy woman to sit her ass down in a chair and wait for me. She can't take the law into her own hands. You hear me Mike? You tell her that and I'll be there just as quick as I can."

Rosie came out of the back room talking on her cell phone. Michael heard her say, "Agent Singleton, it will take you at least forty-five minutes to get here. She could be gone by then. I gave you the address, so meet me at the house. My boss is calling the Sheriff here to assist me."

Not waiting for an answer from the agent, Rosie ended the call, looked at Michael and asked, "Did you get him?"

"Rosie, Sheriff Majors will be here in a few minutes."

"Did he say how long?"

"He told me to tell you that you can't take the law into your own hands. You have to wait for him."

"Michael, I'm going to my motor home to get my gun, I'll be right back. If the Sheriff isn't here by the time I get back, he'll have to meet me at the Larsen house."

"Go get your gun, if that's what you have to do. Then come back here and I'll drive you to the Larsens."

"Michael, are you sure you want to do this?"

"Go, I need to talk with Jessica and Bradley and tell them to watch the place until we get back."

"Thank you Michael. I'll be back in a few minutes."

As she walked to the motor home that was parked in the lot behind the restaurant, Rosie's cell phone started buzzing. When she answered it, she heard Tony say, "Hi sweetheart, how are you? I just heard the news from Juanita."

"Oh Tony, I have so much to tell you, but right now I have to see if I can catch that Paxton woman. She's here in town. I called Agent Peter Singleton in Vegas, and he's on his way. Michael, my boss called the Sheriff and he's on his way here also. I have to go, but I'll call you later."

"Rosie, be careful and don't do anything foolish. Wait for the Sheriff and Singleton to show up. That woman could be dangerous."

"Tony, I've got to go, call you later, bye."

Ending the call with Tony, Rosie then retrieved her old service revolver from the drawer with its shoulder holster and strapped it on.

By the time Rosie returned to the restaurant, the Sheriff was standing in front of "The Egg Stop" talking with Michael, and motioned her to join them.

Sheriff Norton Majors stood about 6'4" and weighed approximately 250 lbs. Even with his mostly gray hair and 60 years of age, he looked very intimidating.

As Rosie approached him, he said, "Young lady, I don't know how they do things back in New York, but in this county, I'm the law and I do everything by the book. Do you understand me? Am I making myself clear? I said by the book. That means I go after the bad guys and you watch period."

Rosie just stared at him for a few seconds and then it was her turn. "Sheriff, I respect the law, and I think I respect you. But if we don't get moving to the Larsens house now, I am going by myself. Do you understand me?"

Michael added, "Sheriff, Rosie and I will follow you at a safe distance so you can do your job without any outside interference from us. Is that okay with you?"

Rosie asked, "Sheriff, where is your back up?"

"Miss Castro, "I have my deputies on the way. They will join me at the Larsen house shortly."

Rosie said, "For now Sheriff, I guess I'm your back up."

The Sheriff answered, "Just stay out of my way Miss Castro, and let me do my job."

Rosie now stared at Michael and said, "Yeah, we'll follow you Sheriff. But if you don't get going now, you'll be following us."

Michael's LTD wagon was parked around back, so as they walked to it, Rosie told her boss, "Michael, I hope that man knows what he's doing. He has no back up other than us, and he's going after a woman who has nothing to lose. We better stay close to him."

Before Michael drove around the building to the front driveway, the sheriff had already disappeared down the road on his way to the Larsens house.

Michael did not know exactly how to get to the Larsen house, so Rosie had to give him directions. Although the old Ford station wagon had plenty of power under the hood, Michael drove as if he was out for a leisurely Sunday drive and was afraid to go over the speed limit.

After being passed on the road by two other vehicles and then another patrol car, Rosie told him, "Michael, I know you like to stay within the speed limit, but please. The Sheriff is way out in front of you somewhere, and now the deputy just flew by. I'm sure he can't give you a ticket for speeding, so please kick this thing in the ass and let's get going."

With that, Michael floored the old LTD and let all the horses under the hood run for the finish line.

Within minutes they were pulling up behind the sheriff's patrol car that was parked in the driveway in front of a large two-story house. The

Deputy, who was driving the second car, had parked in front of the garage and was standing next to his vehicle waiting for orders from the Sheriff.

Looking through the front windshield, Rosie and Michael watched as the Sheriff talked with someone on the front porch. It appeared to be Mr. Larsen.

The conversation seemed to be turning into an argument, and although the words could not be heard, it was obvious that the Sheriff was telling the man from the way he was pointing that he wanted someone from inside to come out onto the porch.

Mrs. Larsen joined them on the porch and started yelling at the Sheriff before stepping back inside and slamming the door behind her.

In a flash, it seemed, the front door opened quickly and the Sheriff took a step backwards. Then two loud thunder-like shots were fired from inside the house striking the Sheriff in the chest knocking him backwards over the railing into the bushes.

Hearing the shots and watching the Sheriff fall, the deputy drew his service revolver and quickly moved to a different position where he would have some protection.

As Mr. Larsen looked over the railing at the Sheriff, who appeared to be dead, a woman fitting the description of Sophie Paxton stepped out onto the porch holding a large revolver in her hand.

The deputy yelled out, "This is Deputy Burns. Drop your weapon."

The woman looked at the Deputy and rushed back into the house followed by Mr. Larsen.

The young deputy slowly moved around the side of the building making his way over to the body of the sheriff. As he picked up the sheriff's wrist to check for a pulse, a shotgun blast was fired through an open window striking the deputy dropping him like a large sack of potatoes.

Michael had already ducked down trying not to be seen and Rosie had opened the car door and slid out onto the ground with her 38 Smith & Wesson in her hand.

Several minutes passed and the front door opened again. Sophie Paxton limped out slowly with a gun in her hand, and walked to the edge of the porch looking down at the two bodies lying side by side. Mr. Larsen joined her on the porch and asked, "What now Sophie? Are you just going to run and leave this mess for us to clean up for you?

Miss Paxton simply said, "Now that's how you get rid of people who are on your trail. You couldn't even stop those assholes in the van with your precious high priced rifle, you fucking wimp."

Moving like a cat stalking its prey, Rosie crawled on the ground out of sight of the two people on the porch until she reached the bushes by the front steps.

Sophie Paxton had already turned around to walk back into the house, when Rosie stood up quickly and said, "Drop the gun Miss Paxton, drop it now, or I'll kill you where you stand."

Looking over her left shoulder and stopping in her tracks, a very cold and nasty smile appeared on the woman's face as she said, "Kill me and you'll never see your granddaughter again Detective Castro."

"But you'll still be dead you bitch," said Rosie.

In her mind, Sophie Paxton must have felt like there was no way in hell Rosie would shoot her as she turned and pointed her gun at the ex-detective. But she was wrong!

Before she had the chance to squeeze the trigger, Rosie's first and second shots hit Sophie Paxton center mass, right between her breasts. The shots pushed her backwards against the wall and the first bullet Sophie Paxton fired embedded itself in the porch column to Rosie's left.

The woman fired a second shot that struck a cement statue on the porch spraying Rosie with nothing more than concrete dust and debris.

Before the old woman could squeeze the trigger a third time Rosie fired another shot entering Sophie Paxton's right eye and splattering portions of brain matter on the house siding.

Watching the old woman fall over as she slid to the porch deck, Rosie still kept her in her sights.

Mr. Larsen had dropped to his knees and was covering his head with his hands next to the porch railing.

Mrs. Larsen watching through the front window as her sister Sophie fell to the floor screamed at the top of her lungs, "Sophie!"

Walking slowly up onto the porch, still with her weapon at the ready, just as she had been taught at the police academy in her early days, Rosie never took her eyes off the woman's right hand with the revolver still clutched tightly in it.

Stepping on Miss Paxton's right wrist, Rosie bent down and removed the gun from the woman's hand.

Next, checking for a pulse on the old woman's neck (which she knew was un-necessary) Rosie determined that the violent woman would never hurt anyone ever again. Rosie's only hope was that the location of her granddaughter didn't just disappear with that woman's last breath.

A crying Helen Larsen came out onto the porch and knelt down at her sister's side.

Mr. Larsen tried to console his wife but she just pushed his hand away and said, "Just leave us alone Stan."

Michael had come up on the porch and put his arm around Rosie and tried to console her.

Rosie said, "I'm okay Michael."

Then she told the Larsens to move away from the dead woman and have a seat on the porch swing. When they didn't want to comply, Rosie lifted her service revolver and said, "I said move it now!"

As they sat down on the swing, a State Police car pulled up behind the station wagon and the driver got out. Seeing Rosie with a gun in her hand the officer ordered her to drop her weapon and place her hands on her head.

Trying to explain what had happened, Rosie said, "I will turn my weapon over to you, but you must keep that pair on the swing covered. They are a big part of this shooting, and I believe the man is the person responsible for shooting my sister and attempted murder of an FBI Agent."

A couple minutes after handing her weapon to the officer, another car pulled into the driveway and Rosie was glad to see the driver when he opened his door and started walking towards the house.

Agent Peter Singleton said, "You couldn't wait could you Miss Castro?

Rosie said, "I'm very glad to see you Agent Singleton. You're right I couldn't wait. After the

Paxton woman shot the Sheriff and the Deputy, I had no choice."

Showing the State Trooper his ID, the agent vouched for Rosie's Identity and confirmed the story she told about the kidnapping. Now they just had to figure out what action to follow.

51

Manual labor was not something Brian Doyle was used to, and it was starting to take its toll on the big man. Having chopped wood for approximately two hours, his hands were red and blistered and his lower back was stiff and sore.

Both little girls had stayed in the cabin just as they were told to do by Doyle. They amused themselves with coloring books, puzzles, cards and games that the kidnappers had purchased.

It was right around lunch time, so fixing something to eat for the girls and him-self, was the next chore he had to do. But since he enjoyed cooking, any time he worked in the kitchen was always a pleasure.

Not hearing anything from Miss Paxton for more than forty-eight hours, Doyle decided to try calling her on her cell phone.

Retrieving his phone from the top of the refrigerator where he had left it earlier, he started to look for Miss Paxton's number when he realized something was wrong. Several things on his cell phone memory had been erased, one of them being Sophie Paxton's number.

Calling both girls into the kitchen where he was seated at the kitchen table, he asked, "Okay girls. Which one of you messed around with my cell phone?"

The girls looked at each other, then Elizabeth started crying and Lisa just shrugged her shoulders and said, "I don't know."

"Now girls, the phone didn't lose the numbers by itself. Someone had to touch it. Now who was it?"

Lisa spoke up and said; "My mommy's phone had games on it, so I was just looking for games Papa Brian."

Hearing Papa Brian brought a smile to the old man's face, and after that he found it hard to reprimand her.

He did have to say something though and he knew it, so he said, "Lisa, my phone is off limits. That means you do not touch it. Do you understand me?"

"Yes Papa Brian."

Doyle said, "Fine. Now you girls go back to playing. I need to call Miss Paxton."

Luckily, the instructions Juanita gave Lisa on how to remove the last call made on the phone was successful and Brian Doyle had no idea that any other calls had been made.

Punching in the numbers and waiting a few seconds, Sophie Paxton's cell phone rang four times and then went to voice mail saying only, "Leave your message and I'll call you back."

"Sophie. It's Brian. Call me back."

The phone call may have been right at the time Miss Paxton was confronting the Sheriff and his Deputy or Rosie, and that's why she couldn't answer, but there was no way of knowing that.

With Agent Singleton's timely arrival and the State Trooper being on the scene, Rosie and Michael sat down on the porch steps and took a well deserved breather. Rosie had just taken a life and no matter how bad the person was, it was still a very traumatic experience.

All of Sophie Paxton's personal possessions would now be in the hands of the FBI, including her cell phone.

The local paramedics from the nearby fire department were called in but all of the shooting victims were dead at the scene and there was nothing they could do but call for the Crime Scene Investigator and County Coroner.

A Sheriff's Deputy arrived on the scene a few minutes after Agent Singleton. He was instructed to carefully bag and tag the weapons in the State Troopers possession.

Rosie gave her version of what had happened and Michael backed it up. The Larsens disagreed and voiced their version.

The Larsens (Helen and Stanley) were taken into custody and were refusing to answer any questions until they talked with their attorney.

A county judge, his Honor Willard S. Blanchard, issued a search warrant for the Larsens' home, garage and surrounding storage sheds.

The search by the additional FBI agents turned up five rifles, two shotguns and six pistols.

The gun cabinet for the rifles in the den had numbered slots from one through six, with each rifle stock having a corresponding number burned into it. But number three rifle was missing.

When asked where the missing rifle was, Mr. Larsen refused to answer.

As the search continued into the second hour, the Larsens' attorney, John Austin, showed up and insisted that the handcuffs that had been put on his clients be removed.

Agent Singleton was just about to accommodate the attorney's wishes when Agent

Selicky walked in from his search of the tool shed, holding a 30-30-bolt action rifle. It had a mounted scope, the same type weapon used to shoot at Rosie's motor home.

Helen Larsen, not able to control her mouth any longer, said, "You dumb ass! You had to keep that goddamn rifle! You're such an idiot Stanley."

The lawyer tried to shut her up, but it was too late.

As they all sat there realizing what had just happened, the Larsens' phone on the end table started ringing, with the caller ID saying Brian Doyle.

After the fifth ring, Agent Singleton picked it up and said, "Hello Mr. Doyle, please don't hang up. Miss Paxton is dead and there is no need for this to go on any longer."

Waiting for a response after a few seconds, the agent then asked, "Mr. Doyle, are you there?"

The silence was broken with a question from Brian Doyle, "And who is this that I'm talking to?"

"My name is Agent Singleton and I am with the FBI. Mr. Doyle. Are the little girls safe?"

But there was no answer. Again the agent asked, "Mr. Doyle, are the two girls safe?"

"Yes they're safe," was Brian Doyle's response.

"What are your intentions now Mr. Doyle, now that Miss Paxton is no longer involved?"

Brian Doyle asked, "No longer involved? You said she was dead. Is she dead or not?"

"She is dead Mr. Doyle. She was shot and killed after she killed the local Sheriff."

"She killed Sheriff Majors?"

"Yes sir. So, I ask you once again Mr. Doyle, what are your intentions with the children?"

"I need time to think. I'll call you back at this number."

As the agent tried to keep Brian Doyle on the phone, it was too late and the connection was broken.

Hanging up the phone, Agent Singleton looked at Rosie and said, "He wouldn't answer, he just hung up. But he said he needed time to think and would call back.

"What about the children?"

"He said they were safe for now, but wouldn't say anymore."

Rosie said, "That bastard."

52

Clipping his cell phone on to his belt loop, Brian Doyle had a glazed look in his eyes when he told the girls to stay in the cabin and stay out of trouble while he goes outside for a short walk to think.

Lisa asked, "Papa Brian, can we go with you?"

Raising his voice a few octaves, he said, "Just do what I told you and stay in the cabin. Do you hear me Lisa? Stay in the cabin."

Elizabeth withdrew into the corner near her and Lisa dropped to her knees, then sat on the floor and started crying.

The aggravated Doyle just walked out in a huff, saying, I'll be back in a while. Stay here."

Walking out to the partially paved road, approximately a quarter mile, the man who at one time seemed so confident with what he was doing with Sophie Paxton, now seemed so lost and confused.

Looking up and down the road a few times, Mr. Doyle turned around slowly and started walking towards the cabin still trying to decide what his next action would be.

He realized that he was now on his own, but also that his location was still not known by the authorities.

Trying to put things in perspective, he decided he needed to check out the essentials for survival since Sophie Paxton and his only means of transportation had been eliminated.

The diesel generator behind the cabin was low on fuel; the dry food supply was also low, and with no way of getting down to the general store, Doyle made a decision to call the store and ask for a delivery for Sophie Taylor, at the hunting cabin.

Calling the local general store and explaining who he was and directions to the cabin, he placed an order.

The food order consisted of all types of canned goods, soup, pasta, sauces, bread, sandwich meats, powdered milk, cigarettes and of course, a couple of boxes of Mounds candy bars.

When he tried to order a fuel delivery, he was told he would have to deal directly with the oil company. Looking up the number in the local phone book that was kept by the phone, Doyle made the call and ordered a delivery to top off the fuel tank.

The fuel truck would be able to make a delivery in four days and that was determined to be about two days before the fuel at the cabin would run out.

Doyle also placed an order for a propane fill-up and he was told he could get that in a couple of days.

Back in Pahrump, Rosie had called Juanita and Tony to fill them in on all that had happened.

Juanita was hysterical after hearing that Sophie Paxton was now dead, and there was no news as to the whereabouts of Lisa.

Tony on the other hand was more positive in his thoughts of the way things were progressing, and was so happy to hear that Rosie was okay after the shooting.

Agent Singleton had called in the appropriate investigating team to make sure there were no screw ups at the shooting scene. The Larsens had been hauled off to the county courthouse jail, for additional questioning and bail for the two had been denied by a very understanding and wise judge.

Rosie and Michael were also brought in to give their statements on what happened before, during, and after the shooting.

An FBI team brought in the equipment to tap and record all calls that came in to the Larsens phone. Along with the most sophisticated equipment for tracing phone calls, there were experts familiar with handling hostage situations.

Unfortunately, no calls other than nosey neighbors and sales calls came in to the Larsen home, and it had been twenty-four hours since the conversation with Brian Doyle.

Things seemed to take a turn for the good when a Sheriff's Deputy, in Delta, Utah, received a call from the owner of the general store near a place called Hiller Mountain.

Elton Shoup, has been the owner of the general store at the base of Hiller Mountain for approximately twenty-eight years, and is familiar with most of the families living on or near the mountain.

Sophie Taylor, as he knew her, was never one of his favorite people. She always had a big, nasty, foul mouth and miserable attitude and now that she was called Sophie Paxton, he was sure nothing had changed.

When he received the phone call from Brian Doyle, and wrote down the list of supplies Mr. Doyle requested, something about the order had a familiar ring to it, but he couldn't place it at the time.

Watching the news that night on the television, there was brief coverage of a woman who had been shot in Nevada who was named Sophie Paxton. She had been wanted along with her accomplice for kidnapping two little girls from New York several months earlier.

Looking at the grainy picture on the television that had poor reception anyway, Mr. Shoup thought to himself how much she looked like the Sophie Paxton that he knew and disliked.

The county post office had "Wanted" posters that they copied and sent out only a month earlier to the local Post Masters. Elton had just put it under the counter along with several other posters and paid no attention to it, until now.

Pulling out the old newspapers, receipts, and unwanted things he had pushed under the counter, Elton found the Wanted Poster and started reading it more closely.

It had the descriptions of Brian Doyle, Sophie Paxton, Lisa Soto and Elizabeth Schorr.

One of the things listed was an uncontrollable liking of "Mounds" chocolate candy bars. Then he noticed the previous names listed for Sophie Paxton.

With the familiar things noticed, Mr. Shoup made a call to the local Sheriff's office and reported it.

At first, the Sheriff's Deputy did not take old Elton seriously. Then he called the Sheriff at his home, who in turn called in the report to the FBI office in Provo, Utah.

The tip from the storeowner was passed on and discussed between other bureau offices. It was considered valid and would be investigated.

Within two hours, a task force had been assembled, but before it would be deployed, an agent would go in undercover and determine if it was indeed Brian Doyle living in the cabin on Hiller Mountain.

Calling the cell number that was given to him, Elton Shoup called and told Mr. Doyle, "Sir, the fuel truck is making a delivery to me today and another just down the road from you. He has agreed to stop at your place and top off your fuel tank, if that's okay with you. Unless of course, you would rather wait until your regular scheduled delivery in a few more days?"

"That's fine. What time will he be here?" Doyle asked.

As Elton looked at the agent who was listening in on the conversation, he said, "He should be there within the hour, as soon as I give him directions to your place, he's a new driver."

Doyle asked, "And the rest of my order?"

"I'll bring that up myself later this afternoon."

"Tell the driver it will be fine, and I'll see you later on then."

Ending the phone call, Brian Doyle had an uncomfortable feeling. It was something about the shakiness in the storeowner's voice that bothered him.

Doyle decided to take another walk back out to the road but this time he had the girls join him on his walk.

Instead of walking down the long dirt road to the paved road, he told the girls that they were going on a nature hike along the path behind the cabin and around the neighboring property to look for deer and other animals.

The girls were happy to be getting out of the house and quickly put on their shoes and jackets.

As they walked the long dirt path, winding around the adjacent property that led them back out to the paved road, Brian Doyle could see a car parked in the clearing just off the side of the road.

As he and the girls got closer, Doyle could see that it was a deputy sheriff's car.

Further down the road he saw a couple of men putting up yellow marking tape and orange cones closing the road to any of the other property owners.

Deciding that something was going on that he was not comfortable with, Doyle told the girls, "We have to turn around and go back the way we came girls. The road is being closed by the police for some reason maybe an accident."

When they returned to the cabin, Brian Doyle told both girls to get in the back room and stay in there.

When asked why by Lisa, the now nervous and angry Doyle, told her in a raised voice, "Lisa, I'm tired of you questioning me. Now just shut up and do what I told you to do. You want to go to heaven when the time comes like all good little girls, don't you?"

Lisa said, "Yes, Papa Brian."

Doyle yelled again, "Then listen to me, and get the hell into the back room."

Both girls walked to the bedroom, and were now crying as they hugged each other while sitting on the bed.

Having a sick feeling in his stomach, Doyle went to the kitchen cabinet and took out the 9mm pistol he had put there when he first arrived at the cabin and placed it on the table.

Removing the rifle from the rack over the fireplace and loading it with shells that were in a storage cabinet near the front door, Doyle felt he was ready for anything now.

As he sat watching out the front window, he saw a small fuel truck coming up the dirt road heading for the cabin.

With the 9mm pistol tucked into the waistband of his pants, but in plain sight, Doyle walked out onto the front porch to meet the truck driver.

Looking more like an office worker than a fuel delivery person the agent got out of the truck and asked, "Are you Mr. Taylor?"

"The name's Doyle, and your name is?"

"Bob Redman, Mr. Doyle."

Doyle said, "The fuel tank is around back in the shed, Bob."

Watching the deliveryman very carefully, Doyle asked, "Are you new at this?"

The driver answered, "Why do you ask that sir?"

"Because you don't seem to know what you're doing, Bob."

"It's my first day on the job sir. I'm a little nervous. Please bear with me, I work in the office. The regular driver came down with the flu, and I have to fill in for him."

Walking back to the truck after checking out the tank location, the driver asked, "So you live here by yourself?"

"Yeah I do. Why do you ask?"

The driver said, "Just friendly conversation."

"I'm not interested in making friends Bob, just fill the tank and get the hell out of here."

"Yes sir I'll do it and get out of your way just as soon as I can.

Doyle asked, "Bob, I noticed the deputy parked on the road. What's going on, an accident?"

The driver thought quickly and said, "I think someone hit a deer sir, the game warden was just pulling up as I asked them to let me through so I could make my delivery."

Going through all the motions for refueling taught to him by the real fuel delivery person, the agent filled the tank and walked up the stairs of the porch where Doyle was sitting, and asked, "How are you going to handle payment for this, Mr. Doyle?"

Doyle looked at him for a few seconds and said, "Wait here and I'll get cash. How much is it?"

"It's $272.40, but a check is okay if you don't have the cash."

When Doyle opened the front door, Lisa was standing there. She screamed and then ran back to her room.

Turning back around to face the driver, Doyle had his weapon in his hand. The driver dove to his left as a shot from the 9mm splintered the railing next to him.

Closing the door quickly two shots from a high powered rifle ripped through the door. Stumbling backwards Doyle went to the bedroom and grabbed Lisa Soto by her arm and dragged her back to the front door. Yelling out loud as he opened the door, "Don't shoot or I'll kill the girl."

Stepping out onto the porch Doyle noticed that the driver was no longer there, but saw him near the bottom of the steps.

As he prepared to fire at the agent, Lisa bit him on the wrist and ran inside as he relaxed his grip.

Before he heard the rifle shot echo through the canyon, he was hit from a shot by an agent with sniper rifle and a scope, who had been watching all the moves of both men and the child.

As Brian Doyle fell backwards into the cabin, he kicked the door closed. An agent called through a bullhorn, "It's all over Doyle, let the children go. Throw out your weapons, there's no need for this to go on any longer."

With no response, the driver, who had jumped off to the side, was now making his way around the side of the building when he heard the children screaming.

The agent, at the side of the house next heard Doyle yell at the crying children, "Shut up you little brats, I need to think."

A full minute passed, then there were two shots in succession, and then it was quiet. One more minute passed and then one more shot could be heard.

Again an agent called through the bullhorn, but there was no answer from Doyle. Five minutes of silence passed and the lead agent knew a decision had to be made.

Not knowing what was going on in the cabin, the driver signaled the other agents to move in slowly after he had looked through a side window. He saw Brian Doyle, lying on the bedroom floor in a large pool of blood.

It took only a few minutes for a team of agents to move in and secure the property around the cabin.

On the command of the head FBI Agent William Powell, four agents entered the cabin.

Walking slowly to one of the bedroom doors, the agent opened the door to find it was an empty room.

Opening the door to the second room, they found Brian Doyle, with multiple bullet wounds and the back of his head blown out. He was lying in a massive puddle of blood in the middle of the room and the girls were nowhere in sight.

Looking around the room, and then under the bed, Agent Peter Creade found both Lisa and Elizabeth, unharmed, huddled in each other's arms crying softly.

First assuring the girls that everything was okay and they were safe, the agent then yelled out, "Suspect down, room is clear."

The cabin and the property were completely searched and through the bullhorn Agent Powell stood on the porch and announced to everyone around the property, "All clear."

As the girls were escorted out of the cabin onto the front porch, the agents and Sheriff's Deputies cheered and applauded.

Agent Powell smiled as he took out his cell phone and called in to his supervisor.

53

Juanita Soto was sitting alone watching TV in her apartment in New York when the call came in from Agent Servantes. Tony was calling to let her know that Lisa and Elizabeth were safe and in the custody of FBI Agent William Powell in Provo, Utah.

Bursting into tears, Juanita couldn't speak for a few seconds. When she did, she asked, "Does mom know yet?"

"I'm going to call her as soon as I get off the line with you. Pack your bags and I'll make arrangements for a flight. You and I are going to Utah."

Juanita said through her tears, "Thank you Tony. Tell mom to call me please."

"Okay, bye."

When Rosie got the call from Tony, she was at work at "The Egg Stop." She too broke into tears. She asked, "Where is she, Tony?"

"Rosie, she is in Provo, Utah, at the FBI headquarters. Agent William Powell and Agent Barbara Hale are keeping both children warm and safe."

"Tony, please get me all the information on where I can pick Lisa up."

"Rosie, I don't know how else to tell you this. Lisa will only be released into her mother's custody."

"Fine, just get me the information where she is, so I can go to her."

"I will. Juanita and I will be flying to Provo as soon as I can make arrangements for a flight."

Rosie asked, "Tony, has Elizabeth Schorr's family been notified yet?"

"From what I've heard, they have been notified. They are making arrangements to fly there and pick her up."

"Thank you Tony. It will be so nice to see you and Juanita."

"I'm going to have a talk with my boss, Rosie, and I'll get you all the information. I will call you back and then I'll meet you in Provo."

Pushing the END button on her cell phone, Rosie just stood for a couple of minutes with tears trailing down her face. She whispered the words, "Thank you, God."

A couple minutes passed, and her phone, still in her hand, was playing her new answer tune, "Cherish."

After getting all the information she needed from Tony, Rosie went into the back room and explained to Michael what her plans were.

First listening to everything she had to say, he then told her, "You're not going there without me. We're a team now." He then hugged her very tightly and said, "Where you go, I go, I've gotten used to you being around, Rosie."

Smiling, Rosie said, "I've gotten used to you too, Michael."

Holding onto her hand, Michael said, "I'm going to miss you if you return to New York, sweetheart. But know this: I'm going to try everything I can to keep you here. Even if I have to tie you up until you decide to stay."

Looking at Michael with a continued smile on her face, Rosie asked, "Why Michael Refino, I do believe your interest in me is showing?"

"Damn, lady, it took you long enough to figure that out. I thought New York women were smarter then that."

"Michael dear, as soon as I get to kiss my granddaughter and my daughter, we have some serious talking to do."

"I may have to consider my options, like a permanent relocation to beautiful Pahrump, Nevada."

Michael told her, "Stop wasting time. You go get ready for the trip to Provo and I'll tell the crew here that they are running the ship until we return."

Rosie asked, "Will you drive me there Michael?"

Michael smiled and said, "Drive hell. I'll call the airport and arrange a helicopter or a plane ride for us. It will be much faster."

54

Because of Michael's knowledge of what a few hundred dollars in the right hands could do, and his love for Rosie, they were boarding a private plane within a half hour after arriving at the Pahrump Airport.

Right around the same time, Tony and Juanita were boarding a corporate jet owned by one of the friends of the bureau chief of the NY branch of the FBI.

Arriving at the Provo Field office around 4PM, Rosie had a hard time dealing with all the legalities involved reuniting with her granddaughter.

Finally after her identity was confirmed, she and Michael were taken to a conference room to sit and wait.

A few minutes passed and the door opened.

Before Rosie had a chance to rise out of her chair, little Lisa Soto, ran to her grandmother crying with her arms stretched out in front of her.

The reunion of Rosie and Lisa also brought tears to Michael's eyes, as he watched from across the table. At that moment, he knew that Rosie would be leaving Pahrump and returning to New York for good. He felt there was no way she was going to leave that little girl again.

Tony and Juanita were ushered quickly to the FBI headquarters, only a few minutes after their arrival at the airport. The parents of Elizabeth Schorr were on the same flight. The emotional connection between the two families seemed to be a bond that would never be broken.

Rosie, Michael, and Lisa, had been moved to a more comfortable room with warmer surroundings, including couches and a TV.

When Juanita and Tony entered the room, the tears were flowing like open faucets, and the reunion was now complete.

Statements would still have to be taken and decisions made. But for now all was wonderful.

It was determined that they would all spend the night in Provo. They would enjoy a meal together and discuss the plans for the future. During the meal at the restaurant that night, Rosie got a big surprise when Juanita announced that she and

Tony had started dating. She was so worried about what her mom would say.

To her surprise, Rosie was more than thrilled when she heard the news. She told Juanita that she too had news to share. She said, "For some ungodly reason, I have fallen in love with Pahrump, and a man who lives there."

Michael sat there not knowing what to say.

Rosie reached out and held Michael's hand, and said, "Unless he's tired of me already?"

Michael gently turned Rosie's hand, brought it up to his lips and kissed it gently, and said, "I love you Rosie."